Kade

THE BRASH BROTHERS BOOK ONE

JENNA MYLES

THE BRASH BROTHERS SERIES

.

For my mom.
Who is the absolute best cheerleader.
I'm damn lucky to have you.

1

BECCA

"Like I told you, lady, there's no apartment for rent here."

The man's brows are lowered, his tone hostile. He's clearly frustrated with me, but I'm too freaked out to care. There are eyes on me. So many eyes. I hate that I'm putting on a show for the whole neighborhood, but I can't just give up. It all has to be a big mistake.

I rush up the last step to the landing, coming within a foot of the man blocking my way into the building. His gray hair is standing on end, pajamas rumpled and hanging crookedly off his frame. He matches the building. It's not the nicest building on the street, but it's definitely not the shittiest. I lower my voice.

"Please, check again. I'm renting a room from Cassandra in Four-B. She's expecting me tonight." I press redial on my phone, hoping that the number I have for Cassandra will magically work. The not-in-service message plays again, and I have to choke the bile down. Keep it together, Becca.

The building manager sighs and shakes his head, a thread of pity coloring his voice. "Lady, Mrs. Cruz lives in Four-B. She's been there thirty years. I been here twenty-three, and I know everybody in this building. There ain't a Cassandra living here." He winces, "You been scammed."

Even as I shake my head in denial, I know he's right. I'd been talking to Cassandra for the last two weeks, but yesterday I sent her my part of the security deposit and first and last months' rent. I sent her $2700, literally everything I had. The bank service fees at the end of the month are going to overdraw my account. Of course, her phone number is disconnected now. She got what she wanted.

The manager's voice interrupts my whirling thoughts.

"Look," he says, his mouth twisted, "You'd better find somewhere to go quick. All that stuff in your car is a big fucking neon sign in this neighborhood."

I can't help but snort. Ya, a gigantic neon sign that says 'gullible fool.'

I glance back at my ancient sedan, filled with literally everything I own. The car and all my shit together are probably worth less than the $2700 I just lost, but I can't stomach the idea of losing anything more.

I've already had everything that truly mattered to me taken away, but somehow the idea of someone stealing my photo albums nearly sends me over the edge, and I have to fight back tears. I'm not a crier. Never have been, so the freaking waterworks are pissing me off. I won't give the eyes staring at me from the windows and from the street corner the satisfaction of seeing me break. I turn back to the manager, dodging the stares from our audience.

"I don't know where to go…I'm not from here." My throat feels tight.

He shakes his head and rubs the stubble on his chin before opening the door to lean further out. "There's a few not too shitty motels about twelve blocks east of here. Try there." He steps back and mutters, "Good luck, kid," as he shuts the door in my face, already heading back to his warm bed.

I try to shut out the gawkers, focusing instead on the wail

of sirens in the distance. This city is too fucking loud. I walk back to my car, head spinning.

How the hell did I get in this position? I'm not a stupid person.

Why did I believe that bitch when she told me she needed the money right away?

As I rest my head on the steering wheel, I have to admit to myself that my decision-making has not been the best since Dad died. I feel like I've been in a pit of pain and grief. I'm only just climbing out of it, keeping my shit together as best I can. I think I did a good job handling the estate, getting the house sold, and the medical bills paid.

Packing up twenty-six years of memories nearly broke me. I kept it together then, but sitting in my car, here in a crappy neighborhood in a city my small-town dad not-so-affection-ately called a *shithole*. I feel like the tape and glue holding all my pieces together are failing.

"One move at a time, Becca," I whisper to myself. "What's the next move?"

I center my breathing the way we did before every martial-arts class, and in a few minutes, I feel calm enough to think. All the cash I have in the world is in my purse. That $374 was supposed to tide me over for the next few weeks while I found a job—preferably one with great tips. But the manager was right. I can't stay here any longer. So much for my fresh start.

The hairs on the back of my neck are already standing up, the same way they did the night Dad's breathing finally stopped. I trusted that feeling and was holding his hand when he passed, instead of crying in my bed. Now, those hairs are telling me something bad is coming for me if I don't move my ass. No way I'll ignore them.

"Okay, motel it is," I mutter, gripping the steering wheel.

I say a little prayer before I start my car, relaxing when the engine only sputters a bit before turning over, checking my rearview mirror out of habit, but I can't even see out the back window. I did the same thing the entire four-hour drive from home. I shake my head and pull onto the street, heading east.

This late at night, the city is dark, but not dark like home. Between the streetlights and the lights from all the buildings, I doubt it's ever truly dark here. I peek up at the sky through my windshield. There's not a star visible in the light night sky.

What a miserable place to live.

Again, I wish I could have stayed in McKinley, but I felt like there was quicksand every step I took there. My friends, all the people I relied on, drifted away, unable to take my pain, my grief. The memories of my life, of Dad, were sucking me down into that pit, and I felt like if I didn't get out now, I wouldn't survive it.

I only make it a few blocks before my heart sinks. My gauges are lit up with flashing warning lights. Please no. I can't handle anything more tonight. A sob escapes before I can rein it in. Jake warned me the car needed work, but I've been praying that it would hang in there. But of course, this is the way my life works now. What's one more hit, right? Life before Dad got sick was…amazing.

Now, I'm walking a damn tightrope.

I scan the street desperately but only see shuttered store-fronts and dark windows. As I stumble through a prayer, I can't help but laugh at what Dad would think of all of this. I can picture his tanned brown face and laughing blue eyes as he shakes his finger at me.

"Plans made in haste, my little Becca, are doomed to fail."

Dad was big on plans. I used to be too. Funny how losing everything you love in a matter of months changes you. Now? Well, I can't summon more than a little bit of panic.

A wet giggle of relief slips out as I see a sign in the distance "Brash Auto." Thank you, Baby Jesus, Buddha, and all the others. My car makes a terrifying chugging/coughing sound before the engine stops. I'm traveling down the street in near silence, the sound of my tires rolling on the asphalt the only thing I hear over my panting breaths.

"Just a little farther. C'mon, car. You can do it."

It feels like it takes a year to roll to a stop in the garage's parking lot. My celebration is cut short when I see it's locked up tight. Of course it is. Why would they be open this late? I still head over to the door and try the handle.

It's locked.

"Well, fuck." I huff out a breath, making my bangs flutter, and take stock of my surroundings.

The night is quiet, only a few cars passing. Around me are more shuttered industrial buildings, and I don't see a single person. The hairs on the back of my neck are laying smooth, though, bringing me a small bit of comfort. My options are limited. I know I could leave my car here and call for a ride, but I hate the idea of leaving everything I have left here without me. Plus, I really can't afford it. It'll be morning before I know it, and I've slept in less comfortable places. I nod as I sort through my options, convinced my plan is the right one. I'll stay here.

I pull my fleece blanket out of the back seat, then crawl back into the driver's and cover myself up. The night is chilly, but thankfully the last hints of winter are gone. *It could be so much worse*, I tell myself as I recline my seat as far as I can.

"I'll be fine, and I'll figure it out tomorrow."

I would almost believe it if not for the exhausted tears escaping my closed eyes.

2

KADE

Ransom's gritty voice over the Bluetooth fills the cab of my truck. "You're wearing yourself out, Kade." He always sounds like he's been chewing on glass, but tonight his voice is rougher than usual.

"We've been over this, man," I mutter as I turn into the industrial area, my shoulders relaxing. I know every building, every crack in the fucking sidewalk here. The familiarity is soothing.

"Yea, we have. We talked about it a year ago. And six months ago. And last week, for that matter." I hear the frustration in his voice. "Fuck, man, you can't keep doing this."

He's right. I know he's right. But I just can't seem to change anything. It's really fucking stupid to be clinging to this little corner of the world when I already own a much bigger one. But leaving here? Leaving everything I know? It's un-fucking-thinkable.

"I don't think I can do it, Ran." I'm uncomfortable admitting it. But I know he already gets it, maybe even more than I do.

His voice slows, gets deeper. "I know how much that

place means to you. It's where everything started for us." His sigh echoes in the dark of my truck. I can hear his frustration with me, and it fucking guts me. I never want to disappoint him, but I feel like that's all I've been doing lately.

"Kade," he continues, "your job is to oversee the operations of all of our garages, not just one. You have a big fucking corner office here with me and a pile of work to do. But keeping the Knight Street location as your office man, running that office too? That's fucking crazy. Hell, it was crazy five years ago. Now? With the way we're growing? You're a damn lunatic." He pauses. "Jonas says you're still handling the books yourself. He says you're being inefficient."

I can hear the smile in his voice as he repeats Jonas's words. Of course, Jonas would use the word inefficient. Nothing offends him more than inefficiency. He's been hounding me to get our expensive custom garage software set up in the shop for years.

I laugh despite myself. "It bothers him so much, Ran. He's been talking about coming to do it himself. I only get him to back off when I remind him that there's actual dirt here." Ransom's rough chuckle bounces through me. He finds Jonas's quirks as entertaining as I do.

Ransom's chuckles die down, "We all have a lot of history there, man. Lots of memories, both good and bad. But Brash Auto corporate needs you. I need you, man."

Ah, shit. There it is. The bastard knows I'd take a fucking bullet for him. We all would. And I know he'd do the same for any of us. I rub my gritty eyes, having only one card left to play. "I can't leave Micah. You know he needs one of us close." There's no way he can argue with that. It's a fact.

"I'll figure something out for Micah. He'll be okay, Kade. I'll make sure of it. But right now, he's not the one I'm most worried about."

I pinch the bridge of my nose and roll my shoulders as he continues quietly. "You look like shit, man. You've fallen asleep at the last four family dinners, and you're losing weight. Keep this up, and we'll be in suits at your fucking funeral within a year."

His voice gets quieter. Deeper. It's his 'try me, mother-fucker' tone.

"This ends now, Kade. You have one month to shift operations to head office. Handle your shit. I will not lose you to fucking stupidity. Not after I've spent the last twenty years keeping you safe."

I pull my truck up in front of the Knight Street Garage and shift into park, laying my head against the headrest and closing my eyes.

"I hear you, brother," I say on an exhale. "I'm sorry I scared you. I'll figure it out."

Ransom grunts, "See you at family dinner. Call me if you need me," then hangs up.

A chuckle makes its way out, despite my exhaustion. Fucker. He never says goodbye.

I dig the palms of my hands into my eyes, wondering how I'm supposed to drag myself away from the only place that feels like home. There's no more putting this off. I know that tone of voice. Ransom will burn the garage to the ground if he thinks that's what it will take to get me out of here, despite the sweat and blood we gave this place. He'd do it in a heartbeat and whistle as he walks away, flames erupting behind him like he's the hero in some fucking action movie. No, there's no getting out of it.

Looking at the shop in front of me, I almost don't go in. My eyes feel so fucking heavy. I could be home in ten minutes and in bed in fifteen. I don't even remember the last time I got over four hours of sleep in a row. There's always too much to do.

But I've built this little prison for myself. I have to get the billing done for tomorrow's pick-ups, or the guys will be fucked. I wonder again, *why the hell haven't I hired a new girl for the front desk?*

The torture of hiring and training is why. I just can't fit it in. I already feel like I'm barely keeping my head above water. But until I do find someone, running the office is on me.

I push my door open with a grunt and climb down, stopping as I realize there's a car parked in front of bay three. I didn't even notice it when I drove in. Too in my fucking head, too fucking tired. The boys know better than to leave cars out front. This isn't the worst neighborhood in the city, but our insurance rates don't need another damn car stolen.

I growl as I head toward it. "Lazy mother-fu…" My muttered curses stutter to a stop as I get a clear look inside, thanks to the security lights on the front of the shop.

There's a person in there.

I bend down to get a clearer look and freeze. Not a person. A woman. Her curly brown hair is covering part of her face, but those lips, no fucking way would god be cruel enough to put lips like that on a man. I lean forward before I even realize I'm doing it. I need to see more. My eyes bounce to the long fingers clutching the blanket under her chin, to the dark slash of her eyebrows, before stopping at the silvery lines on her cheeks.

I back up like she's a snake, rattle up, poised to strike. She's been crying. My pulse speeds up, and I want to turn and run. Why the fuck is a woman sleeping in her car outside my shop? Why was she crying?

I can feel it rising like a flood. My need to fix things, to dig into her life, trying to suck me in, but I force the thoughts down. This is the last thing I want to deal with tonight. I will not get involved in another woman's drama. Between the tears and the fucking car full of shit, she's got trainwreck written all over her, and I don't want to get run over again.

She's got to go.

My heels are dragging as I head back over to the car. *I don't want to do this. I don't want to do this.* It's a constant refrain running through my head. I take a deep breath, then I reach out and bang my fist against her door.

3

BECCA

I wake up with a scream. There, standing on the other side of the glass is a big dark form. I blink quickly, trying to get a better view, but all I can see is a silhouette. The stupid lights from the garage are behind the figure, creating a halo around it.

Crazy thoughts rattle around my sleepy brain. Is this a visitation? Are the aliens coming to get me? Am I gonna get probed? That last thought's not as horrifying as it should be.

I've been in a bit of a dry spell.

My heart is pounding as I drag the keys out of the ignition and slide them between my fingers like pointy brass knuckles. A deep voice startles me.

"You can't park here. You sure as fuck can't *sleep* here. It's time to go. Now."

He's got the kind of voice I normally would love. A voice that would give me shivers while whispering dirty things in my ear. But telling me to leave? Like I fucking want to be sleeping in my car in this deserted area?

Ya, I hate it.

I groan, trying to wake up and gather my thoughts. No

way am I opening this door. I need to slow this down and get my brain firing. Shading my eyes, I roll my window down a crack. "Can you move, please?" I ask. "I can't see you."

I hear him muttering before he shifts away from my door, toward the hood, and 'Hello.' Now that's a man. I'm no stranger to handsome men. I've wrestled around with literally hundreds of them.

But handsome is not the word I would use for this man. Powerful. Chiseled. Intense. Rugged. Those words don't do him justice either, but they're the best I can come up with at—I squint at my phone—2:37 AM. He's got dark hair curling around the collar of his black plaid shirt. His granite jaw is shadowed by the day's stubble. I can see the muscle twitching in his cheek.

Oh, you're annoyed, sexy man? Too fucking bad.

My eyes travel down his throat, lingering at the open V of his shirt before skimming over the powerful arms exposed by the rolled-up cuffs. I fucking love when guys do that. He's wearing dark jeans, the material faded where it strains against his thick thighs.

He clears his throat, and I shoot a look at his stormy face before I pull my eyes away and clear my throat.

"Who are you?" I ask him calmly.

"You're on my property, lady. Who the fuck are you? Why are you sleeping in my driveway?"

Well, so much for calm, cool, and collected. This won't be that kind of conversation, I guess.

Good.

It's not really my forte.

His attitude is getting to me. I can feel the sass rising in my throat, but I suck it back, not quite ready to lose control.

"Ah, sunshine, why wouldn't I sleep here? It just looked so cozy." Great Becca, way to annoy the growly guy.

I chance a peek at his face, and I could swear I see his lip curling up. I can't tell if it's a smile or a snarl.

"You mind getting out of the car?" he asks as he backs up. I snort. No fucking way.

"Not a chance, sunshine. I'm not pretty enough for my disappearance to make the news. Nobody would look for me after you've murdered me." I slap my forehead, then slide my hand down to cover my eyes. Genius Becca, way to tell him you're an easy target.

He coughs. His voice sounds strangled when he asks, "So now I'm a murderer? Why the fuck would I want to murder you? What's in it for me?"

"You could be a crazy sex maniac and want to use my skin to make a dress for yourself. It's the hot guys you have to watch out for, you know. They'll suck you in, make you think you're just gonna have a little fun and bang!" I say, clapping my hands. "You're in a fucking freezer. Not me. No way."

"There's so much wrong with that, I don't even know where to start." He sounds baffled. It's a state many men have been in while talking to me. He's looking at me like I'm some weird new species of eel, turning his head side to side like a new angle will help him figure me out. Good luck, buddy. Many men have tried. All have failed.

He cocks his head. "You gotta pick a new spot to park. You can't sleep here. There are some safer neighborhoods a few miles south of here." He shakes his thumb behind him, then crosses his big stupid muscled arms over his chest like he's solved the problem.

Why the fuck do men do that? Assume I need some big strong man to come up with a plan for me. Like this was really my Plan A? Jesus, I'm on plan fucking X at this point. I let my simmering frustration and anger out to play a bit.

"Oh. Gee. Really?" I say, widening my eyes as I slap my hand over my chest. "You mean I should just start up this car and drive on over to a safer block? Maybe one with nice pretty houses and a nice little park? Why didn't I think of that? Thanks! That's so helpful!" I give him a big smile, loosen my fingers around my keys, and push the key into the ignition.

I lock eyes with him, smiling like a loon while I turn the key. It makes a clicking noise, then nothing. I let my eyes widen and try again. Then widen and try one more time. The tick is back in his jaw.

"Golly gee, mister, my car won't start. What ever shall I do?" I tap my temple with my forefinger. "I know! I'll go park it at a garage so a mechanic can look at it." I look around, acting puzzled, before gasping suddenly and pointing. "Oh my! Would you look at that! A garage!"

He's growling now, but I'm not scared of him.

Which is stupid.

I'm sitting on an empty street with a thin layer of glass separating me from a big, growling man. I should be scared. Maybe my threshold for fear has shifted after everything that's happened in the last six months. Either way, I can't seem to muster up any panic. I'm tapped out.

"Pop the fucking hood," he snarls as he steps to the front of my car. I debate ignoring him, but honestly, it's not like he can make anything worse. And if this is his garage, maybe he can fix it quickly.

Decision made, I reach down and pull the hood release, then slide my feet into my flip-flops. It's a fucking dark street, but the fact is, this guy looks strong enough to punch through the glass if he wanted to hurt me. My gut's never failed me, so I trust it and untangle myself from my blanket, then unlock the door and step quietly out of the car.

I pull my hoodie up and stick my icy hands into the pocket, watching those big shoulders working under my hood. I stand there, staring, listening to him muttering under his breath. The muttering is turning into growls again, and I edge closer to him. He straightens and slams the hood, then steps in my direction before freezing.

His eyes travel over me, from my chipped blue polished toes all the way up over my thick thighs and wide hips, over my never flat stomach, before locking on my eyes. He takes another step toward me, and without thinking, I widen my legs, stepping one foot back a bit, falling naturally into my fight stance. I may not think he's a threat to me, but I would be an idiot to not take some precautions at least.

This guy is huge. I actually have to look up at him, something I almost never have to do. I do some quick mental calculations but figure I can still put him down if I need to. He moves like someone who can handle himself, but not like he's had formal training. I've taken down bigger guys than him without breaking a sweat. Plus, there's frustration and aggression in every line of his body, but every time he lashes out, it's directed away from me.

No, he's not going to hurt me.

My heart's racing again, but it's not fear this time. The way he's looking at me like he'd like a peek under my hoodie? It's…interesting. I pull my eyes from his and quickly tuck the strands of flyaway hair behind my ears, then stuff my hands back into my sweater.

"So," I say, "any luck?"

I already know the answer. My luck ran out a long time ago. He's silent, and I peek up at him again. The man is still staring at me. He looks like someone hit him in the back of the head. Oh, my god. I rush forward and put my hands on his arms.

"Are you okay?" I ask, peering into his eyes.

My first aid flips through my head. Maybe he's having a blood sugar thing? His eyes are locked on mine. His breathing is erratic. I move one hand to press over his heart.

"Are you hurt?" I ask him.

His eyes slide down to my hand on his chest. His body shutters, then he takes a giant step back, away from me.

"Fine." He turns away and runs his hands through his hair. He locks his arms behind his head and stalks back and forth in front of the garage.

I close my fingers over my hot, tingling palms, then slide them into my pocket. What the fuck was that?

4

KADE

W hat the hell was that? My chest is burning where she touched me. It felt like fucking flames racing through me. I can feel her eyes still on me. The biggest bluest eyes I've ever seen.

I can't look at her.

Instead, I pace in front of the garage, trying to convince my cock to settle down. Fucker must be deprived. It's been a fucking year. That must be why he's trying to tear through my jeans.

Jesus, she smells so good. Hints of vanilla and mint. She's exactly my type.

Lush.

I want to taste her. And that pisses me off. This—SHE—is the last thing I need right now. I don't have time for any of this shit. Not the car clearly filled with everything she owns, not the big blue eyes, not the curves for days.

None of it.

Between my work here and the mounds of paperwork waiting for me at head office, I'm already at the edge of the fucking cliff, and the whole damsel in distress thing she has going on is pushing all my buttons. I feel all my old programming rising. Telling me to take care of her, to keep her safe. To do anything for her.

I have to fight it back. I'm not that guy anymore, thinking that if I just do a little more, serve a little more, be a little more, she'll be okay. This woman is not my responsibility.

I grip the back of my neck tighter, using the pain to focus my thoughts. I don't know what the right thing to do is here, but there's no way she can sleep in her car. I can feel my need to understand why she's in this position rising, but I push it back down.

Don't get involved.

Don't get involved.

I suck in a breath and hold it, pretending I'm sitting at the bottom of the pool at my condo watching air bubbles floating to the surface, then slowly release it. I turn to her and meet her eyes. "You can't sleep out here. It's not safe. I'll drive you over to a motel a few blocks away."

She tilts her chin up and crosses her arms over her breasts. I feel my mouth watering like a dog staring at a juicy steak. It's fucking annoying. Why now and why this woman?

"That's unnecessary. I'll stay here. It's almost morning, anyway. What time does the garage open?"

"It's very necessary," I snap. "You're not staying here."

Why isn't she listening? Her reactions don't make any sense. She's clearly in a shitty situation. Why does she look so fucking calm?

As I glance at the inside of her car again, I realize what the problem is.

Ah shit, I'm getting involved.

But just a little.

"I'll cover the motel for the night. And we can move your car around back in the locked yard. Your stuff will be safe there."

She's tapping her chin again, and I feel myself leaning forward, wondering what she'll say next. So far, she's been sassy as hell, and I hate to admit it, but she'd be pretty funny too if it weren't the middle of the night. Her head nods like she's decided.

Finally.

I turn, digging my keys out of my pocket when her voice stops me.

"Nope. I'm not going. Thanks anyway," she says as she opens the driver's door.

I can't stop the words that spew out of my mouth.

"Do you have a fucking death wish, lady? No way you're getting killed on my property. I don't have time to deal with the cops. Get in my fucking truck. Now." I reach her in four big strides and cup her elbow, planning to make her get in the truck. I want to be done with this.

Only somehow, her elbow's not there anymore.

I reach for it again, and she grabs my wrist in a powerful grip. I freeze, surprised at her strength and meet her eyes.

Holy shit.

I don't know what I expected to see on her face. Anger maybe? I'm being a dick, and I know it. So anger would make sense. Fear or worry, maybe? I'm a big guy, and I'm not even trying to use my manners anymore. I'm used to people being cautious around me. Any of those would make sense to me. But no. Her eyes are crinkled up. She's *smiling*.

What the fuck?

She squeezes my wrist. "Aw honey, I'd love to dance. But it's the middle of the night. Why don't we save it for another time?" She reaches up with her other hand and pats me on my cheek, the way Mrs. Marshall used to after I'd repaired her Oldsmobile for the millionth time. From an eighty-year-old, it makes sense. From this woman? I have no idea what's going on anymore.

"You're a fucking lunatic."

She laughs brightly and nods her head before leaning toward me, rising on her toes. She's tall, gotta be almost six feet. Her mouth moves close to mine, and she whispers, "You have no idea, big man."

5

BECCA

The grumpy guy's eyes are wide on me, watching me warily. He should be worried. I'm a woman on the edge here. I think he's finally getting the picture, but maybe I should spell it out.

"I'm not leaving. You don't want me on your property? Fine. I'll roll it out to the street and park there." I'm entering the land of 'I don't give a fuck'. It's been a shitty trip so far, through the treacherous lands of grief and loss, so hopefully I'll get to stay awhile. I open the door, preparing to slide in.

"That's not a fucking solution!" he roars. Roars. Like a big, growly lion.

"Jeez, man. You need to calm the fuck down, or you're going to end up having a heart attack. I really don't want to have to call the ambulance and answer a bunch of questions." I say, repeating his words back to him. I'm joking, but I'm kinda not. He does not look good. "That shade of red is not very becoming."

I slam the door, walking back toward him. He watches me, his chest heaving. I reach out and plant my hand in the middle of his enormous chest and lock eyes with him.

"Breathe with me." I draw a big breath in. He just watches, and I pat him on the chest again. "Breathe. One big deep breath and hold it." I draw another deep breath, relieved when he does too. I hold it, tapping five out on his chest before slowly blowing out. "Good. Again." We do it a few more times, and his colour improves.

I've only known him for fifteen minutes, but I already know he's too stressed.

"You need to center yourself, dude. Give me three things." He looks at me in confusion, and I elaborate. "Tell me one thing you can hear." He studies me, his eyes flipping between mine before answering.

"Traffic on the highway." I tilt my head, listening until I can hear the traffic on the highway far in the distance.

"Good. Now tell me one thing you can smell."

"Vanilla." I smile, liking that one. And a little surprised my body lotion's still hanging in there.

"Now, tell me one thing you can feel."

His eyes sharpen on mine, staring with an intensity that sends a shiver down my spine. It must be the cold.

"Your hand on my chest." I tap my fingers gently on his chest in response.

"Good. Just keep breathing, big man." I let my hand linger on his chest a little longer before stepping back. His hand comes up, trapping mine for a moment, before letting me go.

Now I'm the one who needs centering.

The hum of the garage light. Hints of musky cologne. The breeze ruffling my hair.

I'm suddenly exhausted. I don't want to fight with this man anymore. It's no longer entertaining.

"What's your name?" I ask him quietly.

"Kade Dixon," His voice is still raspy but much calmer than before.

"Nice to meet you, Kade. I'm Becca."

Kade arches an eyebrow. "Rebecca?"

"Not if you want to live to see morning, dude."

A hint of a smile peeks through before he flattens his mouth. "Becca," he says, "you can't sleep out here."

This again. I think I get where he's coming from. But I just can't seem to give in on this. I won't have him pay my way. That's not going to fucking happen.

"We're at a bit of an impasse, Kade. You don't want me here. And I don't have anywhere to go."

Well, that's not technically true, but the idea of calling up one of my acquaintances and begging for a spot on their couch isn't that appealing right now. I don't want to reminisce about Dad. I don't want to talk about the good old days or replay the end for them. I want to put all the pain and the tears away for now. Later I'll pull them out again. When I can't avoid them any longer.

I see him building up another head of steam and raise my hand.

"What do you really want, Kade?"

He pulls his head back in confusion. "I've already fucking told you. I want you gone."

"Okay…but I offered to pull off your driveway. You didn't seem to like that plan. I mean…REALLY didn't like that plan." I leave off the *you roared at me like a rabid lion* part, even though I have a serious urge to poke at him some more.

I haven't had a conversation like this in nearly a year. An interaction that didn't involve measured words, apologies, or awkward, sad silences. It's freeing, talking to someone who doesn't seem to give a fuck about what I think. Or what I've been through.

"You're not fucking safe sleeping in your car. That's a stupid fucking plan."

I have to admire his ability to insert *fuck* into nearly every sentence. I know a few mechanics, most of them love the word too, but he truly is the cream of the crop.

"It's a little stupid," I admit, "but it's not even in the top five stupid things I've done this week." I shake my head at the shit show this week has been. "I'll be okay."

He doesn't look convinced. Not even a little bit. I can see him thinking about ways he can get me to do what he wants. I should save him the trouble, explain to him that a bulldozer couldn't move me if I don't want to be moved, but what would be the fun in that?

Huh. Maybe I'm not tired of fucking with him.

Finally, he sighs, shoving his hands through his hair. "You won't go to a motel." I shake my head no, holding back the smile that wants to escape.

"There's no point. It'll be morning in...five hours." He grunts then turns and walks away, unlocking the door to the office and disappearing inside. "Nice meeting you too," I mutter, a little flustered by the abrupt exit.

It's actually a bit of a letdown. I was really liking the protective, grumpy act he had going on, but I guess it wore thin. Most guys I know back home would be more likely to come to me for protection, than to be protective. I shrug off my disappointment and slide back into the car. It's probably best if I move it off his property, anyway.

The screech of the overhead doors startles me. Through my windshield, I see Kade's powerful body silhouetted as he leaves the bay and heads toward me. My stomach gives a happy flip; he didn't wash his hands of me after all.

He stops at my still-open door.

"Foot on the brake, turn the key on." I follow his instructions. Maybe I should ask what the plan is, but I honestly don't care. He didn't walk away, and I'm too happy about that to question my sudden good luck. I'm due, anyway.

"Foot in," he grunts.

I lift my foot off the pavement and tuck it in, a little puzzled. I hoped we were going to push it into the garage, but maybe we're just going to let it roll back down the slight incline? Maybe he does want me parked on the street.

I shake my head at my foolish hopes, then shift the car into neutral. He cranks down my window, muttering under his breath, then shuts my door and puts his hand on the steering wheel, his other hand on the frame.

"Foot off the brake."

Wait a minute. Is this guy seriously going to try to push this car, loaded with me and all my shit, up into the garage?

Yeah, he is. Apparently without even breaking a sweat.

I realize my hands are hovering over the wheel and drop them into my lap. My help does not appear to be needed. At all. I watch wide-eyed as we get closer to the bay, then sneak glances at Kade's face.

His face is remarkably calm, but I can see the effort in the bunching of his shoulders and the muscles of his arms popping and shifting. His scarred knuckles are white with the strength of his grip. It's got to be one of the sexiest things I've ever seen. His strength and focus. The confidence with which he guides the car into the empty bay, lining up the tires with the lift.

It's all got me a little warm.

"There. Brake." He holds his position until I shift back to park and turn the key off. I lean back in my seat and let my eyes travel up his now relaxed arms and settle my eyes on his.

"What's happening?" I ask quietly.

Kade studies me, gathering his thoughts before answering. "You can sleep in the break room."

How did he go from 'you gotta leave' to 'sleep in the break room?'

"You are a very confusing man," I tell him with wide eyes.

He snorts, mouth turned down. "Nah, I'm pretty fucking predictable." Shaking his head he walks away. "Break room's back here."

I grab my blanket and phone and hustle after him. No way am I going to give him time to change his mind. I'm not willing to take money from him, but a night on the couch inside a building? That's an upgrade I won't fight about.

I catch up with him at the door to the break room. He flicks on the fluorescent light, then moves to the side.

There's an old but clean-looking couch against the far wall, with a beat-up coffee table in front of it. Off to the left is a small kitchenette with a microwave and toaster oven. On the right is a small four-seater table that looks like it came straight out of the 1980s. The whole place looks really clean.

"This is not what I imagined the break room of a garage would look like."

Kade raises his eyebrow. "Not enough grease?"

I smile. "Well yeah! Plus, there are no pinup girls on the walls. I'm kinda disappointed, actually."

"I'm heartbroken," he deadpans.

I laugh, then head over to the couch, giving it a test bounce before dumping my blanket on top. "Thank you for this. Really. I would be okay in my car, but I appreciate the opportunity to stretch out. This body," I say, gesturing up and down, "is not built to sleep in a car."

Kade's eyes travel slowly down my body. He hums, then pushes away from the wall. "Bathroom's here," he says, then moves past it, tapping on the door just outside the break room. "Night."

"Woah! Wait a sec. I have questions."

He freezes, then exhales heavily, shoulders tightening. "Of course you do," he mutters. I wait for him to turn around but resign myself to a conversation with his back when he doesn't.

"Okay. So what time do I have to be out of here? When do the guys get here?" He turns to face me, crossing his arms over his chest again. The glare is back. Why the hell is he glaring now?

"Eight," he bites out. Well, that tone of voice can suck it.

I raise my eyebrow. "Okay. So I'll clear out by seven-thirty. I can go for a walk or something until you officially open. Will the door lock behind me?" The last thing I want is someone walking in on me while I'm sleeping. I feel like I kinda know the grump in front of me, but another guy? No thank you. So getting out before anyone else comes sounds like a brilliant plan to me.

"We have security cameras everywhere."

"Okay…but how do I lock up?"

"I'm not giving you a fucking key."

It's my turn to growl. "I don't want a fucking key. Did I ask for a key? I don't remember that. Do I have temporary amnesia? Quick, ask me who the President is. Oh God, have I forgotten the moves to 'Thriller?'" I put my hands in front of me and do my very best zombie dance. Pretty sure it looks nothing like the original dance moves, but it's the best I've got considering I got kicked out of dance class in the first grade for giving Lukas a black eye. Little perv was trying to look up my skirt. What else was I supposed to do?

Kade's voice interrupts my dance. "You really got a mouth on you, huh?" He's looking at me like I escaped from an institution. I'll take it over the mean, suspicious look he was wearing before.

"I have a low threshold for jackassery," I tell him honestly. "It's sarcasm or making people bleed. Sarcasm is easier on my clothes."

"Yeah," he mutters, "I suppose it would be."

He takes a few steps toward me. "I'll be working in the office all night. You don't have to lock up." Then turns and heads back into the garage. I hear the squeal of the overhead door again and wait a few minutes before sneaking back to my car to grab my pillow.

As I make a sleeping bag out of my blanket and snuggle in, I can't quite decide why the idea of him being just a few feet away while I sleep is comforting. There's just something about him. I giggle quietly, thinking about the look on his face when I told him I couldn't dance with him, then drift off to sleep.

6

BECCA

At 7:30, my alarm goes off. I stretch out, wiggling my toes, appreciating all the room. This is so much better than sleeping in the car. I'm toasty warm and feeling well-rested, even though I only got a few more hours of sleep.

I throw back my blanket and slide my feet back into my flip-flops before padding as quietly as I can through the service bays toward the front office Kade disappeared into last night. I need to pack up my bedding and pee, but I just can't resist the urge to get my eyes on him. I wonder if that pull I feel toward him will still be there in the light of day. It was weird. He was pissed, and grumpy, but somehow, I felt more alive in the minutes we spent together than I have all year.

My heart flips as I stop in front of the window separating the room from the garage. It's clearly a waiting room for customers with a door to the outside near the front window and another door next to me. There are a few chairs, piles of magazines on a small coffee table, and a dead plant in the corner. Across the room is the service counter with a computer set up on it, and past that, tucked at a desk in the corner, his head resting on his folded arm fast asleep, is Kade.

I stare at him the way I couldn't last night. Most people look relaxed when they're sleeping, but not Kade. The line between his brows is deep, and his jaw still looks tight. The hand on the desk is clenched. I rub my chest, wondering why this man looks like he's about to fight a battle, even in his sleep. What happened to him? I want to know more. I want to know it all, and I can't help but shake my head and laugh a little at myself.

I thought it was all crap.

When I was little, I would swoon when Dad would tell me the story of how he met Mom. He always said it was like a bolt of lightning hitting him, and he knew he would do anything to make her his. As I got older, that story just made me sad. Dad didn't get much time with Mom before she fucked right off. I never saw him date another woman. I wonder if he felt like it was worth it, loving someone so much only to have them walk away. And if he wished that bolt of lightning had missed him.

My eyes well with tears as I realize I already have the answer to that question. I wouldn't trade a second of my time with Dad. I would live every moment over again, even knowing the pain I would feel after he was gone. And last night, I realized his story about the lightning bolt, well, it wasn't crap. Because I felt something last night.

As I watched Kade grumble his way around the garage, clearly not wanting me here but completely unable to walk away from me until I was safe, a feeling washed over me. It wasn't a lightning bolt. It was a slow-growing awareness. A wondering.

"Who you?" a deep voice says from behind me.

I scream and flip around into a fighting stance, ready to defend myself.

And yep, I pee a little.

7

BECCA

W ell, that's embarrassing.

The massive guy standing there takes a big step away from me, glancing from side to side. Looking for a way out, I assume.

"Sorry!" I yell. "You scared me." Woah. Gotta lower the volume a bit. "I mean, hello, good morning. How are you this fine morning?" I give him an awkward wave.

His eyes are still darting side to side, and his hands tighten on the strap of his duffel bag. Jesus, do they make all the men here giant? This guy is as big as Kade, maybe bigger. His golden skin makes him look like he spends all day in the sun. He's wearing blue overalls with a sewed-on name patch. I look back at his eyes.

"Micah? Is that your name? I'm Becca."

He's still backing up. Crap. This man is not responding to my usual in-your-face energy.

I drop the manic smile from my face and soften my stance. "It's okay, Micah. I'm sorry I yelled. Have a good day."

I back up a bit and relax against the wall of the office. Micah briefly meets my eyes before walking in a wide circle around me. He watches me from the corner of his eye until he disappears on the far side of the garage. The light shifts, and I turn my head to find Kade in the open door of the office. He's looking off where Micah disappeared.

"I'm sorry I made him uncomfortable," I say, wondering what I did to chase him off.

Kade nods his head, but his eyes are hard. "It's fine."

I study his face. "You don't look like it's fine."

Kade rubs his jaw before answering. "Micah's a little different. You didn't do anything wrong."

I nod. I know there's more to it, but Kade's face has shut down. It's clear we're not discussing this further.

"I'll look at your car, then let you know what I find. Just… wait for a bit." He waves me into the empty waiting room.

I salute him with a smile. "Yes, sir!" then wander past him into the office and sit down in one of the customer chairs. I pull my hood up, cross my arms over my chest, and slide down into the chair. Might as well sit here for a while and worry about how screwed I am if the repair is as expensive as Jake said it would be.

Kade's boots stay pointed at me for a few more seconds, and he whispers, "Sir," in a way that makes my lady bits happy before he walks away. I worry for a few more minutes before getting sick of myself, raising my head and examining the room around me instead.

What a mess.

It's obvious it's a bunch of guys running this place. Judging by the layers of grime on the top of the empty water cooler bottle, I'm guessing it's been months since this room was cleaned. It's weird. The rest of the shop is spotless. All the tools are clean, the floors are wiped. Hell, even the break room I slept in was taken care of.

But here in this office? It's been completely neglected.

I peek through the window into the garage and see two sets of legs near the hood of my car. I'm sure the guys will be occupied for a while, and I've never been good at being idle.

May as well make myself useful for a while. It's the least I can do to repay him for letting me sleep on the couch last night.

I'M UP ON A CHAIR SCRUBBING THE DIRTY WINDOW WHEN I HEAR Kade walk back into the room. I had to strip off my hoodie ten minutes into the cleaning, so I'm only wearing my white *Tyler's Brazilian Jiu Jitsu* tank top and my black leggings. He says nothing, and I can swear I feel his eyes boring into my jiggling ass. When I can't take the tension any longer, I look over at him.

Yep. Staring at my ass.

"Yo! Eyes up here, big man."

He startles and snaps his eyes back to mine. I smirk and raise my eyebrow but don't say anything else.

"Ah…Um," he clears his throat, "What are you doing?"

"You know that brown stuff all over the office? The stuff that gets all over your clothes and makes you sneeze? That's called dirt," I continue in a sing-song like I'm teaching a kindergarten class. "And do you know the best way to get rid of dirt boys and girls?" I scrunch up my nose, wondering if he'll play along.

"Clean it," he answers in a monotone voice. But I can see the twitch in the corner of his mouth. He's playing.

I clap my hands excitedly, "Oh, that's so good, Kade. Great answer!" I laugh, completely enjoying myself. I turn back to the window and give it one last wipe before hopping down off the chair.

Kade raises his arms and steps toward me, then stops and folds his hands behind his back. Humm. Was he going to catch me? The idea of jumping into his arms and flattening him like a pancake makes me smile. But then again, he's pretty damn big. Maybe he could catch me. I'm considering jumping at him to see when I notice the scowl is back.

Shit, this is not going to be good.

"You can say it. The car's fucked, isn't it?"

He sighs and looks down. "Yeah. It's fixable. But it's going to be about three grand to get it fixed up right."

I tilt my head and consider him. That's not what Jake had told me. The repairs were going to be more like five thousand. No way would Jake ever pad the bill or take advantage of me. We'd peed in kiddie pools together as kids. We're good as family. So three thousand? Kade is definitely discounting the bill. I hum in the back of my throat. There he goes again, trying to give me money. He's being sneaky about it. Why would he do that for a woman he doesn't know?

"I don't have three thousand dollars," I admit.

Kade nods slowly. "Yeah. I figured." He exhales a big breath and tucks his hands in his pockets, raising his shoulders. "I'll cover the cost. It's going to take a couple of days to get the parts and get the work done, but you should have it back before the weekend."

Just like that? I could be on my way to…what? My plan, moving to Chicago, was half-assed to begin with. Now that I have no place to stay, it's looking even stupider.

More stupid.

Stupidest.

Whatever.

When it comes right down to it, I have no idea where I'm supposed to go, or what I'm supposed to do next. This being a grown-up shit is for the birds.

Kade looks at me expectantly, like he's anticipating my *yes*. Jesus. Who is this man? Who does that? Just give a stranger three grand like it's nothing. Not to mention the hours they'll have to spend to fix it. I take a moment to find just the right words.

"That's really generous of you, Kade. Really. I don't know what to say except…no fucking way." I smile and nod at him. Kade's shoulders drop, his eyes widen, and his mouth drops open.

"I…What?"

"I'm sorry. That came out wrong." He relaxes again, and I continue, "No fucking way are you fixing my car and paying for it yourself. Thank you very much for the offer, though."

His mouth is open again. The poor guy looks so confused.

"Did you actually think I'd say thank you and just let you pay?" He nods slowly at me. I tilt my head. "Huh," I say, considering him, "Am I safe in assuming I'm not the first damsel in distress you've helped?"

Kade's face shuts down, and I have my answer before he mutters, "No."

"Gotcha."

He's got a hero complex. Last night is making a lot more sense. He actually couldn't walk away and let me be. I wonder why?

"Well, taking handouts from strangers isn't really something I do. I clean up my own messes." Admittedly, this mess is big, but I always handle my shit. Always. I don't actually have a clue how exactly I'm going to do that, though.

I think better when I'm moving. Running in place, I sort through my options. "It's probably not worth fixing. It's a fifteen-year-old car." I stop to chew on my pinkie nail, but my jittery legs force me to keep moving. "I've got a little bit of cash. Maybe I can find a hostel. Or couch surf. But shit, where do I keep my stuff?"

I'm vaguely aware of Kade's bobbing head in my peripheral vision.

"Maybe a hotel for a few days? But then what? I'll have blown through the cash I have before I know it. Even if I get a job with great tips, it'll take me forever to save up enough to pay another first and last month's rent. Agh! Fuck you, Cassandra!" I finish dramatically, shooting both middle fingers up to the sky.

Kade's voice sounds strangled when he asks, "Who's Cassandra?" I stop jogging and swing toward him.

"She's a lying, thieving, conniving fucking bitch." Kade's face looks kinda sweaty. "You okay? You look a little warm." I hide my smile and jump a bit. Yep, his face goes blank and gets redder, and his eyes lock on my chest.

"They're nice, huh?"

Kade clears his throat and shakes his head. "What?"

"My boobs!" I jump again for emphasis. "See!" I have to clench my teeth to keep from laughing. His head is bobbing every time I jump. Thank you, stretched-out sports bra.

Kade shakes his head. "What? No. Yes. Fuck."

He covers his eyes for a minute and takes a deep breath that stretches his T-shirt across his chest. Now I'm staring.

"Can you focus, please?" Frustration colors his words.

I nod and let my smile slip out. He narrows his eyes at me, then clears his throat.

"Okay." He draws the word out before continuing, "Cassandra. She's a bitch. Why? What's she done to you?"

I don't want to tell him. I don't want to admit it to this put-together man. This man, who can spend three thousand dollars on a stranger without a second thought and has tires on his truck worth more than my entire car. But what would be the point of lying? I pull my big girl panties up, push my shoulders back and look him right in the eye.

"She's the woman who conned me out of twenty-seven hundred bucks." I press my palm to my forehead. Fuck, now I'm sweating. "I paid her first and last and a security deposit. We were going to be roommates. But when I got to the building…well, she doesn't live there and never did."

He raises his eyebrows and whistles through his teeth. How do guys do that? I spent the entire summer between fifth and sixth grade trying to learn how to whistle like that.

I passed out three times.

"Well fuck. Thieving bitch is right." He takes a step toward me. He's stopped looking at me like a puzzle. Instead, he looks…angry? "And her number's not in service, right?"

I nod. He shakes his head, walking over to the desk and grabbing paper and a pen, dropping them on the reception desk between us. "Write down any information you have for her. How you first connected, names, phone number, email. Anything you have." His eyes are blazing, a deep V arrowing between his dark eyebrows.

"What are you going to do?" He looks like he could fly into a rage. It's kinda hot.

"Me? Nothing. But my brother Declan can find pretty much anyone with just a phone number." A little thrill goes through me at the idea of tracking that bitch down. I wouldn't mind getting her blood on my clothes.

"I...that's really kind. But I can't ask you to do that. I'll figure things out on my own."

8

KADE

I wonder what it would take to get her to jog around a little more. Christ, the way her breasts bounced around in that tank top just about gave me a fucking heart attack. This woman just keeps surprising me. When I walked into the office and saw that spectacular, round, wiggling ass, I just about swallowed my tongue. Mesmerized, it took me a second to register what she was doing.

I don't know how long it's been since the windows were washed. She's done more cleaning in thirty minutes than I have in the last four months. The guys take care of the back, but I would never ask them to clean up front. And her little lecture about dust. Jesus, I'm torn between wanting to know what else she'll say and wanting to kiss that sassy mouth.

It's pretty clear that she's not who I thought she was. She's down on her luck, yeah, but she's not desperate. She's not broken yet.

I'm so fucking relieved she's okay.

And I'm really worried about how relieved I am.

I keep trying to remind myself that this woman is not my problem, but it's not sticking. She's nothing like I expected, and the fact that I'm drawn to her doesn't seem like such a bad thing anymore. She's not like them.

I think.

I need more time with her to explore this thing. This fucking feeling. A feeling I've never had, not with any of the women I've dated. I need a little more time to figure this out. And yeah, make sure she's back on her feet. So I come up with a dumb fucking plan right there on the spot. "Look. You've had a run of complete shit luck, right?"

I'm so stupid. I should shut up now.

She nods. "You have no idea."

Shit. Now I want to know more, but I set that aside. "I get it. You don't have many options right now. I'm guessing you don't have a credit card you can use to get a motel room for the month?"

Her head shaking doesn't surprise me. If she had other options, she wouldn't have been sleeping in her fucking car.

"Right. Okay. We might be able to help each other here."

Sure Kade, invite her right in. While you're at it, might as well hand her the keys to your truck and your wallet. That's where this is going to end. It always does. But I'm helpless to stop it. She's already sucked me in.

The way her eyes narrow at me tells me that my word choice has put her on edge. A gentleman would put her at ease right away. I'm no fucking gentleman. I slide a smirk onto my face and lean in. "Maybe we scratch each other's backs…you know what I mean?" I wiggle my eyebrows to up the creep factor. Her eyes narrow, skipping over my face. The look on her face…it's too good. I crack and can't hold my rusty laugh in.

"Dickhead," she mutters. But she's smiling.

"Sorry," I sputter as I wipe my eyes. Christ. Not that funny, but I've been under pressure for so long that it's like a valve being released. I can feel my body relaxing in a way it hasn't in months.

I straighten up and look at her face. She's still smiling at me. God, it lights up her entire face. That fucking perfect face. I wonder what she looks like when she wakes up in the morning, all soft and warm? That thought sobers me, and I put a little more room between us. "Shit. I'm sorry. I was fucking with you a little."

My smile fades as I look at her. I shuffle through a few stories I could tell her to get her to agree to my plan before realizing the truth is just pathetic enough to work. Something tells me she won't fall for a story anyway, and she's already shown she won't take any favors from me. Though, I'm painfully aware she could be working a long con. It wouldn't be the first time a woman targeted me.

"I'm fucking drowning," I admit to her. Her smile is gone, but her face is still so open. "I haven't slept over four hours a night in more than a year. There's too much work for me to keep going the way I am."

I hesitate before speaking this last bit of truth to her. I haven't admitted it out loud to anyone.

"I've been popping antacids like they're fucking candy. I think I'm getting an ulcer."

Her eyes are warm, and she takes a step toward me, her hand raised like she's going to touch me, before lowering it to her side. I want her to touch me more than anything else. I shake off the random thought and focus on my mission. Laying it on thick. But it's the truth. Real and unvarnished.

"You're in a shitty spot. I need help. I mean, look around," I say, gesturing to the piles of paper covered in dust. "It's pretty obvious things have gone to shit in here."

"I noticed," she says, looking around the room again.

"Yeah. Well, I had a girl upfront here for a while. But she moved, and I haven't had the time to find someone new."

"So, what exactly do you need help with?" Her curiosity chasing the suspicion out of her voice.

"Answering phones. Invoicing customers. Collecting payments and ordering parts. Talking to the fucking customers. All the shit I don't have time for, but that keeps this place running."

She bites that juicy lip of hers. "I haven't worked in a garage before."

I nod, knowing she'd have to be a fucking unicorn to have shown up in my driveway fully trained. "Have you done anything like it?"

She's studying me, considering her answer. Considering me. My skin is prickling under the weight of her stare. "I started working in the office at my dad's Dojo when I was twelve. I was handling the whole business side by the time I was fifteen."

The breath whooshes out of me, and I nearly fold over. Thank fucking christ. Though honestly, she coulda told me she was a coke dealer, and I probably still would have hired her.

I'm that fucked up.

"Then you can do this job. I can show you our systems and teach you how to order parts. Hell, all the guys here can help with that. What do you think?"

She bites her lip and tucks her hair behind her ears before answering. "You really need the help?" I'm nodding before she even finishes the question.

"Yea, I do."

"So, how would this work?" she asks tentatively.

I hide my smile. I've hooked her. Now to reel her in. "I'll pay you the going hourly rate for an experienced shop manager. We'll get you set up upstairs this morning, then you can start this afternoon." I like the idea of knowing exactly where she is. That she'll be safe. I know I'm inviting chaos into the office, but I can monitor the business side of things and find her fuck ups before things get too bad.

"Set up upstairs?" she asks with a raised eyebrow, suspicion lacing her words.

Tread carefully, Kade. "There's an apartment upstairs. It's been empty for a long time. I've crashed there once in a while when I was too tired to go home. It's basic, more of a studio than an apartment. But it's functional. And it's safe." It was a fucking refuge. For all of us.

Becca's eyebrows are almost in her hairline. Her face red, arms crossed, fingers tapping on her arm. "I don't need your charity."

I shove my hands through my hair in frustration. Why is she so fucking difficult? Every other woman I've met jumped at my help. Hell, they asked for more, and more again.

Until they'd bled me dry.

Emotionally at least. I have way too much money for them to be able to take it all, though they did give it a damn good try.

"It's not fucking charity. It's a place to stay for a while. It's an easy commute to work. And it's sitting empty."

She doesn't look convinced, so I push her.

"What other options do you have, Becca?"

Crap. Her eyes are glassy. She swallows, and I want to take it back. Yes, I need her to stay, but I don't want to hurt her feelings.

"You're right. I don't have many good options." She exhales. "But I won't stay in a free apartment." She raises her hand to cut off my objections. "I'll pay fair market rent." What the fuck? I don't like it, but I nod my agreement as she continues, "Let's do a two-week trial. If things don't work out, we'll go our separate ways."

"A month," I counter. "Two weeks is barely long enough for you to get your feet wet."

"Three weeks." I open my mouth to object, but she crosses her arms and arches an eyebrow. Her sharp, "Take it or leave it," shuts me up.

"Fine," I mutter. "Let's get your stuff unloaded and upstairs." I hide my smile as I head toward her car, satisfied with the outcome.

Checkmate.

9

BECCA

I wander around the apartment after the guys leave, running my fingers over the furniture as I explore. There's a layer of dust on everything, but not nearly as much as in the office. This place is small but bigger than my place in Tokyo. And I shared that apartment with two other women. The bathroom was the size of a Porta-Potty. Mornings were a nightmare. The bathroom here is at least double the size.

I take a quick peek at the fridge to make sure it's working. I already ate everything I'd packed in my small cooler. A grocery run is going to the top of my priority list after work today. I wander over to the queen mattress pushed against the far corner. It's sitting on a frame with no headboard. It looks like it belongs in a dorm room or a teenage boy's bedroom.

Kade pulled new sheets out of the cupboard, so maybe I should get the bed sorted first. When I pick up one of the pillows, I can smell him on it. He's been crashing here more than 'once in a while,' I think. It makes me feel better about my decision to take the job. I don't want him to feel like I'm taking advantage of him, especially since I kinda want to get to know him better.

I change the sheets quickly, except for the one pillowcase, which is a little creepy I admit, then spend a few minutes in the bathroom washing up. I look tired, dark circles under my eyes, but there's nothing I can do about that. It is what it is. I use water to smooth the flyaways back into my ponytail, pat my round cheeks, then head out.

The entrance to the apartment is at the back of the garage through the locked gates. I have to admit, being behind an extra layer of security makes me feel a little better about this arrangement. The door has a good solid lock, but I'm not stupid enough to think Kade gave me the only key.

I wonder if he understands how much trust I'm putting in him. A single woman taking a job and an apartment from a strange man is the way a horror movie would start. This could be one of the stupidest things I've ever done in my life.

But I still can't bring myself to regret my decision. I want to be here. I'd choose working in a place like this over waitressing any day. And honestly, I don't have the temperament to work in a restaurant.

Too much politeness. Pretty sure I'd end up with hives after the first shift.

Plus, I want to be around Kade. Which is so stupid to even think about, considering I met the man hours ago. But there it is.

Everything I know about him so far tells me he is a good man. And a man who needs me. Well, needs me in his office at least. I've never really been needed by anybody before. Dad loved having me around, and he gave me lots of jobs to do, but I always knew he could've done them just as well himself, until he got sick that is. Now, having to learn a new business, spending time doing something completely different from my usual routine, is a great distraction from the grief.

This feels different. This feels like the start of something new. Something big. I have nothing to lose, even if he turns into a colossal asshole and I walk away in a few weeks.

And it beats waiting tables. Let's face it. I'd end up punching somebody.

When I return to the garage through the back door, I feel like I've entered a new world. When Kade took me upstairs, he, Micah, and I were the only people in. Now I count at least five other guys in coveralls working throughout the five bays. I spot Micah in the bay furthest from the office and head toward him. He sees me coming but says nothing. I stop next to him and examine the car he's working on.

"Man, what a piece of shit." I mutter.

Micah hums but doesn't respond. This guy is a tough nut to crack. With his help, we'd unloaded my car in about fifteen minutes. Each man carried more in one trip than I did in three. Even so, I didn't get a peep out of Micah and that just makes me more determined to figure him out. I have a feeling I'll have to work for it. Still, I've never been able to walk away from a challenge.

"Why would someone fix a car as trashed as this one?"

Micah straightens and looks straight into my eyes. "Love," he says simply before turning and walking away.

Love?

Mysterious bastard.

I want to be him when I grow up.

THE REST OF THE AFTERNOON FLIES BY IN A BLUR. KADE TEACHES me the accounting program and how to order parts. We help a few customers. The work itself isn't hard, but Kade's presence is a huge distraction. He's always looking at me. Brushing my arm or my back. Leaning close to show me something on the screen. It's driving me nuts. I would think it's accidental, but there's something in his eyes telling me it's not. Or maybe that's just wishful thinking.

I've had boyfriends before, but this level of awareness of hypersensitivity is completely new. It's like my body knows exactly where he is at all times. Like little threads of electricity are running between us. It's weird, and wonderful, and I want more of it.

I hand the last customer of the day their keys, then lock the door behind them. I'm tired, but my body is humming. Leaning back against the door, I lock eyes with Kade.

"You did good, Becca. Fuck, better than good," he says with a smile. That smile. Jesus. The way his eyes crinkle up. I'd gotten a lot of those today. The scowl hadn't made an appearance all afternoon. This version of Kade, the smiling one, is a hell of a lot more dangerous.

"You have dimples." *Oops. Off-topic. Danger, Danger.* "I mean…thanks. The systems are fairly simple. Other than, you know, the whole car thing," I wave my hands toward the garage bays, "it's pretty close to what I did before."

His smile's gotten bigger. "Working for your dad, right? What made you leave and come here?" I lean my head against the door but keep my eyes locked on Kade.

"He died."

The words land between us like a lead weight.

Kade's eyes tighten in sympathy. He swings his legs off his desk and drops them to the floor. "Fuck Becca, I'm sorry." He's leaning toward me, looking like he's waiting for me to dissolve in a puddle of tears and snot.

"Thank you," I reply automatically. I've heard I'm sorry so many times since he passed. It seems like it should help, should dull the ache, but it never does. It's still as raw as ever. "It doesn't seem real sometimes. I pick up my cell to call him almost every day."

"How long has he been gone?" he asks softly.

"Six months. He was sick for three months before he passed away, so we had a little warning. I got to spend all my time with him." I blink quickly, trying to push back the tears.

I don't want to cry right now, especially not in front of Kade. He rises and walks toward me, stopping with the tip of his big work boots an inch from my sneakers.

His eyes are so warm.

"You handled everything yourself? What about your mom? Brothers and sisters?"

I shake my head. "It was just us."

"Ah, honey. You're all alone," Kade murmurs before opening his arms. He slides his hand behind my shoulder and gently guides me to his chest. Coming from him, it's unexpected. But not unwelcome.

I let myself fall into him, not at all interested in trying to act tough and put together. As Kade wraps his arms around me, I feel the stress of the last twenty-four hours...hell, the last nine months bubble over. He pulls me into his chest, and I rest my ear over his heart. I feel his stubbly chin catch my hair where he rests it on the top of my head.

Our bodies are plastered together from the knees up. I keep my eyes closed against the tears and instead focus on Kade's slow, steady heartbeat.

I didn't realize how much I needed this simple comfort.

All the people back home would give me quick hugs and awkward sympathetic smiles. I don't know what they were more uncomfortable with, death or my devastation at losing Dad. Either way, it felt like they couldn't bear my grief and would pull away too soon. I would have done anything for a hug like this when Dad died.

The slow, gentle circles Kade is rubbing on my back. The big powerful arms holding me tightly. It feels like he would stand here for as long as I needed. I let myself soak it in, memorizing the cadence of his heartbeat, the whoosh of his breath, the rise and fall of his chest, the spice of his skin, before slowly pulling away.

His arms tighten for a minute before unwrapping.

I step back and take a deep breath before meeting his eyes.

The warmth is still there on his face, but so is something else. Something that makes my belly clench.

"Thank you. You're great at that," I tell him. "Gold star!"

I'm such an idiot.

The corner of his mouth curls up. My head feels fuzzy. I slide out from between him and the door and make my way back to the counter, tidying up already tidy piles of paper. He's leaning on the door now, watching me.

"I ah, think I'll head up. Thanks for today, Kade."

He's watching me like I'm a problem he's trying to solve. I feel more nervous words bubbling up, but I clamp my lips together to hold them back. He watches me for days more before nodding and pushing off the door.

"Get your purse. Let's go." I'm grabbing my purse from behind the counter before he even finishes. I briefly wonder what else I would do, without question, if this man asked me to, but I drag my mind out of the gutter.

"Where are we going?" I ask, but I don't really care. I'm not ready to go up to the empty apartment.

"Food. I'm fucking starving."

I smile at him. "Food sounds good."

Kade leads me to his truck, opening the door for me to jump in. I didn't know guys still did that. I resist the urge to bow or do something equally awkward, giving him a small smile instead.

I feel completely out of place as I look around the luxurious leather interior. It's expensive, the chrome accents are shiny, and it's so, so clean. There's not even a speck of dirt on the floor mat. I wonder what he thinks of my ancient, messy car. What he thinks of messy me. I smooth my hands over my hair before tucking my hands under my armpits so I won't leave fingerprints.

"We're just grabbing food. You can stay here if you'd be more comfortable. I'll bring you back something." Kade's voice snaps me out of my spiral of embarrassment. He's twisted in his seat, looking at me. The tick is back in his jaw.

"I…I'm comfortable."

I'm so not.

I wish he drove a rusted-out pickup with dust everywhere. How does his truck stay so clean while the office gets so dirty? It doesn't make any sense.

"Don't fucking lie to me. You look like you're afraid I'm about to drive you out to my murder house." His words are sharp, clipped. His anger stabbing at me, jolting me out of my thoughts. Jesus, his attitude flipped fast. I throw my hands up and twist to face him, taking in his cold eyes and hard face.

"Woah, dude!" I have to laugh. "Looks like we both have our heads up our asses.You're over there, thinking I'm a scared little chick terrified of you. Meanwhile, I'm over here trying not to dirty up your perfect, worth-more-than-my-old-house, truck."

I snort and shake my head at our mutual stupidity before leaning forward, pressing my fingers on every surface I can reach in the truck. It takes a while. Kade's watching, unmoving, as I mark everything up. I settle back in my seat.

"There, that's much better." And it is. It's not shiny anymore, fingerprints and smudges marring the once pristine dash and door. A bit of embarrassment creeps back in.

"I…uh…didn't realize my fingers were that dirty."

Shit. I really am an idiot.

Pulling the sleeve of my hoodie over my hand, I buff the door, but Kade's first chuckle stills my frantic movements. The chuckles roll from deep in his chest, one after another. Waves of sound crashing against me. He's leaning back against his door, left hand gripping the wheel. His whole body is shaking with his laughter. It really is the best sound. If I could listen to that sound the rest of my life…well, I wouldn't be mad about it.

I wrap my hands tightly over the strap of my seatbelt,

holding myself back. I want to crawl to him and press my chest against his so I can feel the laughter roll. And maybe lick him a tiny bit. There, on the corner of his smiling mouth. Kade's laughter dies as we sit, caught in each other's eyes. Electricity zapping between us.

His fingers tighten on the steering wheel before he yanks his eyes from mine and clears his throat. "Pizza okay?"

I nod, unable to look away from him. I'd go eat caterpillars off the trees with this man, as long as he keeps looking at me like that.

10

BECCA

I am in over my head.

The whole way over here, I was trying to tell myself that this feeling would settle down. That this attraction I feel toward Kade is not as big as I'm making it out to be. That it's just relief over having somewhere to settle for a bit.

But those butterflies in my stomach have morphed into big, hairy mutant moths careening and colliding in my whole body. Maybe they're morphing because we no longer have the distraction of work between us.

The colliding, the brushing, the casual touching we did today, and the slow, gradual buildup of sensation have put me on edge. Looking at him now, relaxed in the booth in front of me, sipping his beer, eyes on me, the nerves are back in full force.

"Ready to order?" The harried waitress, Sue, her name tag reads, smiles at Kade. It's clear from the extra attention she's paying him he's a regular here.

Kade nods his head at me. "Large pizza, whatever she wants on it."

I briefly consider pushing him to order what he wants, but

it's pizza, and I'm starving, so nah. "Sausage, mushrooms, onions, olives, and fresh tomato, please."

Sue jots it down and takes the menus, leaving Kade and me to sit in tension again. My eyes are skittering around the restaurant, cataloging the couples on dates and the families wrangling their kids. It's clear from the line at the door that this is a popular place.

"So, um, you come here a lot?" Shit. Real original Becca.

Kade smirks before taking another sip of his beer. "Yea. Pizza's good, and it's close to the shop."

"Good. That's good."

Kill me now.

I swear I've had conversations before.

With men even!

But usually, a conversation goes both ways, and Kade doesn't seem to be that interested in speaking. I'm tempted to pull out my phone and distract myself, but I can almost feel the slap my dad would give me if I did that.

"Why are you smiling?" Kade's looking at me intently.

"I didn't realize I was." I let my smile grow and admit to him, "I don't really know what to talk to you about, so I was thinking about getting my phone out."

"And that's funny how?"

"My dad hated cell phones. HATED. He had a flip phone for work, but he refused to buy me a smartphone. When I finally bought one on my own, I had to sit through regular lectures about how technology was creating a disconnected society." God, those lectures! I swear I know them all by heart. "If I picked up my phone when we were at dinner, he would slap my hand. Not a little slap either, a big one. It would echo around the room, and everyone would look. It was so embarrassing!" I chuckle, enjoying the memory. It became a game for us.

When I look up, Kade's face is dark, his brows pulled

down. "He hit you?" he asks in the coldest voice I've ever heard from him. Startled, I lean forward as I explain.

"Well, yeah. But not the way you're thinking."

He doesn't look convinced, and the idea of him thinking what he's thinking about my dad breaks my heart a little. I lean forward, pressing my chest into the edge of the table.

"My dad was one of the most dangerous, capable people I've ever met. I watched him make more than one grown man cry. But he would never hurt me. A slap on my hand once in a while though? Well, that was to make a point." Kade looks a little less like a thundercloud, but still pushes.

"Parents shouldn't hit kids."

"Agreed," I whisper. I rub my chest before asking the question I don't think I want the answer to. "Did your parents hit you?"

He leans back against the cushion of the high booth and studies me before slowly nodding his head. "My mom hit sometimes. I didn't know my dad." Anger is coursing through my body. From his tone, I think his mom hit him more than sometimes. But he looks like he's put up a brick wall. Still, I can't help digging a little.

"Why did your dad leave?" I don't like the smile that comes over his face. It looks old and tired.

"My mom didn't tell me much about him." He shrugs. "Knowing the type of men she went for, I doubt I'm missing much."

"My mom bailed when I was little, too." It's a shitty thing to have in common.

"Did you ever meet her?" he asks with a frown.

The arrival of our pizza saves me from answering. I don't really want to talk about my mom with my hot boss. My stomach lets out an embarrassing growl as Sue sets the pizza down in front of us. Pretty sure Kade heard that. I look up at the waitress.

"Sue, you're an angel. This looks amazing!"

She leaves us with a kind smile, and I waste no time diving in, pulling three slices off, cheese stretching from the pan to my plate. I bring the full plate to my face, inhaling the intoxicating blend of tomato and spice and ooey, gooey cheese.

"Oh sweet Baby Jesus, that's the best smell in the world."

Kade's snort briefly distracts me from the amazingness on my plate. I shoot him a grin before focusing back on my pizza.

"Dude, you better dig in. I'm not some delicate little woman. I ate a whole large pizza once on a dare. And I don't mind trying again. I didn't get this ass eating salad."

He shakes his head at me with a reluctant smile before sliding a few slices on his plate. We're both silent, busy inhaling our supper. After my second slice, enough to partially satisfy my growling stomach, I stop to watch Kade eat, trying not to stare. He's eating the way most athletes I've met do. Big bites. Barely chews. Too hungry to stop and appreciate the food in front of him.

As I'm watching, he stops to pull an olive off and drops it on his plate to join the others already there before polishing off the slice. Huh. I rest my chin in my hand and study him openly. His eyes catch mine as he's reaching for another slice.

"What?" he asks with a frown. I study him for another minute.

"You don't like olives."

"No."

"Huh." That's telling.

Kade's frown deepens. "What?"

"Why didn't you ask for no olives then?"

"Cause I can pick the little motherfuckers off."

I smile but keep pushing. "Yeah. You're doing a great job of it, too."

Kade raises his eyebrows. "Why are we talking about this?"

I shrug. "It's just interesting."

The tick is back in his jaw. "Interesting? Olives are interesting?"

I shake my head. "No. Olives are delicious little salty pieces of heaven. What's interesting is you telling me to order and not speaking up for what you want." Kade's shaking his head again, looking completely baffled.

"It's fucking pizza, Becca. Again, why the fuck are we talking about this?"

"When you come here with friends or order it for the shop, do you ever get the kind of pizza you like?"

I've known this man less than twenty-four hours, but I think I have him figured out. He's a caretaker, always making sure the people around him get what they need. He answered question after question at the shop today, handling things that he could have easily passed on to one of the guys. Always taking on the load.

"No," he bites out, clearly done with this conversation.

"That's what I thought," I mutter as I grab another slice. So good. I pack it away, pretending like he's not watching. No way will I let his stare ruin this magical pizza for me.

Kade's still staring as I sit back with a sigh, gazing longingly at the rest of the pizza in the pan. I'm too full for more. I meet his eyes and cock an eyebrow at him. I wonder if he's used to people caving and spilling all their secrets when he glares like that. But I've faced down bigger, scarier guys. He thinks he can pressure me?

Nah, time to fuck with him.

I take a deep breath. "What? You've never seen a big girl eat before? I will not allow you to shame me for eating." I shake my finger at him, pleased when his eyes widen and dart around the restaurant. "Just because I have thick thighs and a round tummy does not make me less deserving of pizza." I have to bite my lip from cracking at the look on his face as I slap the table and raise my voice. "I am a big, thick, juicy woman. And life is too short to not eat the pizza. So fuck salads! Fuck judgment!"

A woman's "Amen, Sister!" from a few tables down cracks me up.

Kade looks so fucking confused.

"I…" He's shaking his head as he leans as far away from me as possible in the small booth. "I wasn't…I would never… You eat whatever you want."

"Okay," I say with a big smile as I take a long sip of my water, locking eyes with him. It's worth the wait to see the realization slide over his face.

"You're fucking with me."

I smile bigger and wink at him. "Yep. I owed you."

He chuckles a little, and despite the laughter in his truck, it still sounds rusty. I decide right then and there to make it my mission to hear it at least once more tonight. He sighs and looks at the pan

"You want any more?" he asks. I shake my head, and he hesitates. "Are you sure? I really wasn't judging…"

The giggles rock my shoulders as I hold up my hand to stop him.

"Kade, I really was fucking with you. I'm full. That's all. I love my body. I think it's perfect. And anyone who doesn't think so can go fuck themselves."

My giggles stutter in my chest, and Kade's eyes slowly travel over my body, lingering at my throat and breasts before meeting my eyes. I swear he mouths the word "perfect."

A flush travels up my neck in reaction to the heat in his gaze. I've seen that look before. And I want more of it. The man wants me, and the feeling is completely mutual. I stare back at him, letting him see the heat, the want in my face.

I've never been good at flirting.

I'm more of a hit him on the head and drag him back to my she-cave kind of woman.

Not that I've done that very often either. I always tried to keep a professional distance at tournaments, and honestly, it wasn't that hard. No one really appealed to me, and the last thing I wanted to be labeled as, was a whore. Stupid double standard. But people talk, and the tournament circuit is a small, gossipy world.

But here, with Kade? Well, my dirty thoughts are putting me a little off balance. And he's my boss. So climbing over the table into his lap is probably not the right move here. But I can't bring myself to brush off the way I'm feeling. Or even hide it. It's too interesting, too rare, and I don't want to. If the last year has taught me anything, it's that life is too short to hide from the big things. Big feelings, big adventures, big life.

Sue's approach interrupts the moment. "Can I get you guys anything else?" We both shake our heads no, and Kade settles the bill. I don't argue. He said it was his treat, and the man can clearly afford it.

As he slides out of the booth, I realize I'm not quite ready for this to end. To go back to my little apartment and stare at the walls. I don't want to be alone with my thoughts or my feelings. I hesitate but decide to ask

"Kade," his eyes slide back to me, still sitting in the booth. "Any chance you could take me to a grocery store? I had a couple of things in a cooler for the drive. But…" My words drift off as his face hardens.

He nods and waves me out of the booth. "Let's go."

THE LAUGHTER, THE HEAT AT DINNER feel like a distant memory. The air in the truck feels heavy and cold, the tension between us snapping tight. The ice coming off of him is really confusing.

"We can skip the grocery store. I'll go tomorrow sometime."

"It's fine," he bites off, not looking at me.

It's clearly not fine, judging by the "fuck you" in his tone, and I waffle between trying to start another conversation and jumping out of the truck. I can't really afford a trip to the hospital, so I search for a new conversation topic before remembering something that niggled at me all day.

"Kade, does Micah use ASL?"

Kade glances sharply at me. "Yeah."

"And you use it too?"

He nods but doesn't say anything.

"Did you learn when you hired him?"

Kade shakes his head no, and when he doesn't follow it up with anything, I resign myself to a silent ride.

I want to know how he knows sign language. I want to know everything about him, but I'm going to have to live with the disappointment.

At least I know a little more about Micah. Maybe I can watch a few videos, figure out what signs Micah might use the most. Maybe he'll write out a list for me. I'm going to ask him first thing tomorrow morning.

I grab a cart at the grocery store, conscious of Kade's dark presence at my back. I thought he would stay in the car, but maybe he needs a few things too? Deciding to ignore Mr. Grumpy Pants, I head off around the perimeter of the store, grabbing enough fresh food to last me the week, but at the meat department, I realize I'm missing some key information. I sneak a look behind me and see Kade standing in the middle of the aisle, arms crossed, cold eyes fixed on me. Right.

"I forgot to check," I say softly. "Are there pots and pans in the apartment?"

Kade's nod is glacier slow, and I spin back to ponder the meat. I blink back the wetness in my eyes and look for any discount labels.

My excitement over the new job, over Kade, is waning. Based on the hostility on his face, it's unlikely I'll be employed much longer. I've got to make every penny in my wallet count.

I grab a discounted package of ground beef expiring tomorrow and a few other inexpensive cuts, then veer into the middle aisles to pick up a few pantry staples. By the time I get to the checkout, I'm fried. Both from the mental stress of adding up every item in my cart as I shopped and Kade's scowling presence behind me.

The man ruined grocery shopping for me.

Fucker.

I quickly unload my cart, chatting with the tired guy at the register. He's young and looks like he's about to fall asleep where he stands. Poor kid.

"That'll be ninety-six seventy-four," he says, the squeak in his voice making me smile. I'm fumbling with my wallet when from the corner of my eye, I see a big tanned hand holding a card heading toward the debit machine.

"Aaagh!" I yell before flinging my body between the hand and the machine, wrapping my arms around the little pole it's mounted on. As I glance up, I see the kid's wide eyes locked on my chest. I peek quickly and exhale in relief when I see the girls are still strapped in right where they should be. My eyes shift to the tanned hand, frozen a foot from me, and follow it up to Kade's face.

His face isn't cold anymore. In fact his eyebrows are about to disappear into his hairline.

"Becca…what are you doing?"

"What am I doing? What are you doing?"

His eyebrows lower again. "Paying for the fucking groceries."

"What the hell for?"

He blows out a frustrated breath. "Can we finish up here, please?"

I nod. "Sure." Kade moves toward the POS machine again, so I lean more of my weight on it, pressing my boobs harder onto the number pad. Kade's growl makes the hairs stand up on my arms.

"Move Becca."

Asshole thinks he can growl at me and get his way?

Better set him straight right the fuck now.

"You are not paying for my groceries, Kade. Back. Up." I make sure every bit of ice I can gather is in my tone.

His eyes flare, and his body rears back. The hand holding his card drops to his side. I shift so my ass is blocking him as I fish out my wallet one-handed and drop it onto the counter. I grab five twenties and slide them over to the kid, not taking a full breath until the change is in my hand. Only then do I straighten up.

I smile my thanks to the kid then loop the bags over my fingers, satisfied with my haul. I swear I've spent a hundred bucks at a grocery store before and only left with one bag, so I mentally pat myself on the back, proud of my shopping prowess.

Maybe I should take up couponing. I've watched those shows. I could have a stockpile. Maybe I should get my own apartment first. Then stockpile.

I spend the short walk to the truck trying to figure out where I can find coupons and wondering which online couponing groups I should stalk. Kade's arm reaches past me to open the back door for me, snapping me out of my thoughts.

"Thanks," I mumble, sliding the bags off my fingers onto the floor. I push the door shut and turn, colliding with Kade's chest. His hands come up to wrap around my biceps. His fingers are nearly touching. My arms are strong, muscle wrapped with a nice warm layer of fat. Seeing his fingers wrapped around me drives home his strength, his size.

"Sorry," he says as he drops his hands.

My eyes meet his briefly before shifting away. "It's fine."

Kade reaches for the door handle, and I hop in with a quiet "Thanks." My heart is racing, and the tingles are back again. I pinch my thigh, muttering to myself. This is so stupid. The man is giving me fucking whiplash, but my stupid body doesn't seem to mind at all. She's all in for this ride, stupid hussy.

It takes me a minute to realize we're not moving. Kade's in the truck, his warmth radiating toward me, the only sound in the cab the deep in and out of his breath. I exhale and tuck my hands under my thighs before glancing at him. He's studying me, looking so serious. I don't get it. I'm not that complicated.

"You're giving me a complex Kade," I mutter. He tips his head in confusion. "You go from…" I hesitate, unwilling to say *smoldering sex god,* "…friendly to cold as ice." I shrug and throw up my hands. "It's really confusing."

He's still staring, and I'm a second away from turtling into my hoodie when he speaks. "Micah and I grew up together. We learned ASL together."

I lean toward him. Dammit. Bastard hooked me again.

"We watched videos and used books from the library." He clears his throat, and his change in subject rocks me back in my seat. "I thought you expected me to pay for your groceries."

"Why?" I breathe.

"Because you're fucking homeless, Becca."

"Bullshit." I glare at him. "You know I'm not."

"You were sleeping in your car."

I throw my hands up, frustrated. "For one night, Kade!"

He pulls his eyes from mine and rubs his hand over his stubbled jaw.

"What do you see when you look at me?" I want to know.

He blows out a breath, his eyes jumping around, hesitating. "A woman who needs help."

I nod, disappointed but not terribly surprised. He looks at me and sees a problem.

Maybe I'm imagining the heat, the want.

Maybe it's wishful thinking.

"Right." I tuck wisps of hair around my face behind my ears. "You don't really know me. But I think you need to know something." I wait for his eyes to meet mine. "I'm actually a badass."

A condescending smile inches over his face as he looks at me. "Sure you are."

Huh.

He doesn't believe me.

I wonder why.

The thought makes me giggle-snort. I realize I'm a fucking disaster right now. But I'll pick myself up again. I know exactly what I'm capable of, so I don't doubt myself, even if Kade does.

11

KADE

W ho is this fucking woman? She's charmed everyone we've interacted with today, from the grumpy old bastard arguing over his repair bill to the waitress at the pizza joint to the squeaky-voiced teenager at the grocery store. All of them got sucked into her orbit.

Hell, so did I.

And I'm pretty fucking pissed about it.

I wanted her to stay. I wanted her safe, but I didn't expect I'd get so obsessed. With my history, I should really rein my shit in.

"Goodnight," she whispers at the door.

I nod and hand her the last grocery bag. She let me pay for the pizza, but the way she argued with me about paying for her fucking groceries? Christ, I've paid more than her grocery bill for a shave. I can't say I'm particularly proud of that, but when you have as much money as I do, you sometimes buy stupid shit.

My smile creeps back, picturing the way she dropped her body over the debit machine, blocking me. She fucking won that one. Her eyes are wide now, shining at me from the dim apartment. I lock my hands on the doorframe to stop myself from grabbing her.

"Do you want to come in?" she whispers. I really do. Her eyes are wide, warm, and friendly. But I'm too fucked up to handle this. To handle her and not lose myself. I'm already way too fascinated by her. If I spend any more time with her, I'm going to be fucked. I shake my head.

"Nah, it's late. See you tomorrow." I turn and bolt down the stairs. I stop and look up at her, still standing in the doorway, loose hairs curling around her face. "Lock the door, Becca."

The softness has fallen away from her face, leaving disappointment in its wake. As I watch, the disappointment slides away, replaced by a rueful smile. "Message received, boss. Goodnight." My body locks up as the finality of those words sink in. She softly closes the door. I wait to hear the lock before jogging to my truck. I double-check the gate and doors before jumping into my truck.

"FUCK!" I yell, punching the roof of the cab.

What the hell am I doing?

I started this. I maneuvered her until I got her to stay, and now I'm regretting it. I wasn't supposed to feel this. This obsession. This ache. Her hooks are digging into me. I already feel panicked at the idea of leaving her here alone tonight. I'm worrying if she'll be okay. If she'll be warm enough. If she'll need anything. I want to take care of her.

I've known this woman twenty-four hours, and I already feel like I'm losing the man I've worked so hard to be this last year. No way am I going back to being that person. That doormat. The one who gave and gave and gave. The one who believed every promise. Who tried to put her back together every time she fell apart. I can't let myself get dragged down.

No, it's obvious that I need to take a step, or twenty, back. It's better for everyone.

. . .

THE NEXT DAY AT WORK, I FORCE MYSELF TO KEEP MY DISTANCE, physically and emotionally. She takes the lead in the office, looking like she's been doing it for years. Everyone who walks in the door gets a sunny smile. All the mechanics make excuses to come in and visit with her.

I warn them away at first, but it's like trying to hold back ten dogs after one ball. Becca seems to handle them just fine, though. Laughing and joking with them like she's known them forever. I hate that she laughs and teases them.

She doesn't brush up against me like yesterday.

She doesn't smile at me or talk to me at all other than the odd question here or there.

I tell myself it's better this way. That I don't miss her light. And I definitely don't ask her any more about her past.

I know if she ends up sad or teary again, I won't be able to stop myself from holding her. I can't be the one to fix this broken woman.

I'm not capable of fixing her without breaking myself.

12

BECCA

My three-week probation drags by. I get to know the guys in the back, and Micah and I develop a system to communicate. He wrote me out a list of common words for the garage, and I've been watching videos to learn how to sign them. He lets me practice on him, laughing when I screw up.

He actually said three words to me yesterday 'Thank you, Becca." When he speaks it's slow, hesitant. Never more than a few words. So it may be a small thing, but it feels like a big victory somehow.

There's something about Micah that makes me want to take care of him. To shelter him somehow. Which is weird considering he's got at least sixty pounds and six inches on me, and I am not a tiny woman. But he doesn't avoid me anymore. Even letting me sit near him while he works on his cars. He doesn't even seem to mind all my questions, answering them with a couple of words each time.

It took me way too long to figure out that he does something very different from the rest of the guys in the garage. They're all working on cars that go in and out daily, their owners coming for them within a day or two. But Micah's doing restorations, working on three cars for the entire time I've been here, only jumping in to help the other guys when he's stalled waiting for a part.

It's been satisfying seeing something so neglected come alive again. I feel like I've been coming alive again too. Coming back to the person I used to be. One not so weighed down by grief. I twirl in my chair again, leaning my head back to watch the ceiling spin by. The office is quiet today, leaving me alone with my chaotic thoughts.

It's D-Day.

I'm not looking forward to telling Kade I'm leaving, but it's pretty clear that's the right path for me.

I've taken to walking in the evenings, unable to sit and ponder my life and my choices. And yes, the disappointment over Kade freezing me out has me sick of myself. I built up this thing between us in my own mind, and I feel dumb still thinking about it.

So when I came across a Dojo late last week during a walk, I couldn't resist going inside. It smelled like home. That mix of sweat and mat cleaner was so familiar. When I saw Devin at the front desk, an old friend from the tournament circuit, I nearly burst into tears. "I didn't know you opened your own place."

I laughed and hugged him. His husband, Jeff, came around the corner, and we all hugged. They were so kind and insisted I come and train. It felt amazing to be back, moving and flexing my body. I was starting to feel like myself again.

The me before everything exploded.

By the end of the week, they'd offered me a job. I didn't even hesitate before saying yes. It felt right being there. Like I'd found a home again. With people who know me but didn't witness the unraveling of my life. A place for my fresh start.

The clatter of tools and muffled cursing from the bays brings my attention back to the office. I hop up and head into the garage toward Micah, waving at the other guys as I pass them. I plop onto the low stool next to the workbench and watch him work in silence for a few minutes. He's bent over working in a previously empty engine compartment.

Earlier this week, I watched from the office window as Kade and Micah worked together to get the engine in place. Both had shrugged out of the top of their coveralls, leaving them in white T-shirts with the coverall arms tied around their waists. Both men were big, strong, muscled, and sweaty. Any woman would happily watch them for hours. Micah is bigger, more muscled, but my eyes were drawn to Kade again and again.

I'd barely seen him the last few weeks. He'd come into the office a few times, but only briefly. I'd texted him a few times with questions, and he always got right back to me, but he brushed off any attempt I made to connect with him again. I could swear I still felt that electricity. Like he was watching me, wanting me. But he never got close. It's pretty clear that he's shut the door on more, and I'm feeling pathetic, mooning over him and getting nothing back. I know leaving is the right decision.

"Kade…here," Micah rumbles, as always a careful pause between words so he doesn't stumble over them.

I glance up and out the open bay door and see Kade climbing out of his truck. He's wearing dress pants again today, and a white-collared shirt, the top three buttons undone. I wonder if he looks like that all day or if he yanks off his tie at the end of the workday. I'd seen him in that kind of outfit a few times, but I still wanted to climb him like a tree every time I did.

Stupid hormones.

I tear my eyes away and focus back on Micah.

"How the hell did you know that? Your head's been in that engine this whole time. Be honest, Micah, you're a bit psychic, aren't you?" I tease him.

I hear the humor in his voice when he grunts back, "Good…ears."

I laugh and glance over to see Kade in the office, watching me. "Catch you later, Micah," I say, then walk slowly to the office, Kade's eyes on me the whole way.

Avoiding his gaze, I move across the office and hop up on the reception desk. I swing my legs, gently kicking the desk with my heels, looking past his shoulder, watching the cars go by on the street out front. The air in the room gets thicker.

"It's been three weeks," I blurt suddenly.

"Yea, it has." He seems to be waiting for something, unwilling to say anything more. I exhale, my chest feeling heavy.

"I've found another job," I whisper. "It's a few blocks away at …" I stutter, to a stop at Kade's growl. My eyes snap to his burning ones. He's glaring at me like I've done something wrong. A little flame of anger ignites in me.

"You can stop glaring anytime now, Kade. We agreed on three weeks, and if it wasn't working, we'd move on. Well, I'm moving on." My breath is coming faster, my heart pumping.

"What's not working, Bec? This place is running better than it has in years." Scowling, he pushes his hands through his hair, leaving it standing straight up. "Years Becca. Why the hell would you want to leave? Am I not paying you enough? I can up it."

I'm shaking my head. "No. It's not that. I…I need something different. I'm not used to sitting in an office all day. I just thought this would be different. That's on me." I give him a sad smile. "I'm sorry. I'll stay on for a bit and help you get someone new trained. I can do both jobs for a little while."

I really do feel bad. While this isn't my dream job, I know I'm letting my personal feelings get in the way. But I don't want to stay here and feel this pull every time I see Kade. It's like being at Wonka's chocolate factory and not being allowed to eat—or lick—anything. And having him avoid me at all costs is not good for my ego. It's better to go, and find some guy who wants me as bad as I want him.

He's pacing back and forth, muttering. Better to finish this now. "I'm hoping you'll let me rent the apartment for another couple of months, just until I've got enough saved up for a new place."

He spins to stare before demanding at me, "Where? Where are you working?"

"I found a job at the Dojo a few blocks away. I can walk there easily enough. It's mostly later in the day, so like I said, I'll still work here for a while."

My hands are twisting in my lap. I honestly didn't expect him to be this upset about me leaving. This is not the reaction of an employer losing an employee. I can't resist asking, "Kade, I'll help you train someone new. You won't be left with everything on your plate again. Why are you so upset?"

He freezes, except for his hands, curling and uncurling reflexively. His jaw is flexing, and his eyes are still burning into mine. The tension ratchets higher as the seconds tick by slowly.

"Fuck it."

I jump, startled by the sharp words. Before I realize what's happening, his arms are wrapping around me, his hand threading through my hair, angling my chin up, and his mouth covers mine.

I'm surrounded by him. Taken over by him. By his soft lips. His seeking tongue. His stubbled cheek scraping my soft one. His hips pushing between my legs. His arm banding around my back, pulling me closer, tighter. My swirling thoughts coalesce.

I'm fucking pissed.

This asshole basically ignores me for three weeks, and now he's kissing me. Fuck that. I'm going to give him a piece of my mind.

In a minute.

But first, I'm going to make sure he knows what he's been missing.

I weave my hands up through his arms, grabbing his shoulder and hair, pushing into his kiss. Biting, then soothing the sting. Teasing and chasing. Breathing him in. Learning what makes his breath stutter in his chest and what makes him growl. The growls reverberate through my chest, making my breasts tighten. I want to take more. I want to grab his ass and pull him closer, so he can rub me just right, but no.

Just as suddenly as he grabbed me, I push him away, grab the edge of the counter, and lift my foot, planting it in the middle of his chest, holding him back before he can grab me again. He wraps his hands around my foot, eyes dazed, and pushes forward, but I hold strong, surprising him.

Is he surprised because I stopped his kiss or because I'm strong enough to hold him back? We're both panting. His hair is standing up. I think mine is too. Our eyes are locked, and my inner hussy briefly considers hauling him up to my apartment so I can muss him up some more. But I set it aside and let the flame of my anger ignite into a blaze.

"What the fuck, Kade? What the hell was that?" I ask him, my words clipped and fast.

His slow grin and slower words enrage me. "Well, baby, that was a kiss. I can demonstrate again if you'd like." He's rubbing his hands slowly from the top of my foot up to my ankle, playing with the strip of skin between my socks and leggings. There's no controlling or containing my anger now.

"Stop!" I yell, kicking him away. "Just stop it." I swear there's a red mist over my eyes.

Kade takes a step toward me, and I roll backward on my shoulder, over the desk, landing on my feet on the other side. My stupid mouth and my Office obsession take over, and I can't resist as I straighten up. "Parkour," I whisper under my breath.

I smooth my hair, then pull my anger back over me like a blanket, meeting Kade's dumbstruck eyes.

"Who the fuck do you think you are?" I ask him quietly. I see the wariness come into his eyes, the realization dawning. "You've ignored me for the last three weeks. And what, you're suddenly overcome and can't take being in my magical presence for one more minute without kissing me?"

He nods slowly, eyes locked on me. "Yea, pretty much."

"Bullshit," I spit the word. "No fucking way are you allowed to treat me like that. I liked you, Kade. I wanted to spend time with you. Get to know you. And you completely shut me out." I'm the one pacing now. "What did you think was going to happen here?"

"Honestly," he admits carefully, "I hadn't gotten that far."

I really don't like that answer. It makes me sound like I'm some impulse to him. "Then why, Kade?"

"Because the idea of you leaving pissed me off."

Entitled dick.

"Right. So you're pissed off. And your reaction is to kiss me? Kissing someone without their consent? That's assault, asshole." I cross my arms, glaring at his stupid, beautiful face. God, it could have been so good between us. But he had to run away, and now he's ruined it.

He stumbles back a step. "Fuck, Becca, no. That's not what I meant."

"No? You didn't mean to angry kiss me?"

His hands are rubbing through his hair, back and forth. In his eyes, I see regret, apology, and shame. His chest deflates as he drops his hands.

"How did I fuck this up so badly?" I don't think he's asking me. Kade steps forward and plants his hands on the reception desk, separating us. We're facing off, both in turmoil, both lost in our emotions.

"Becca," he starts, dropping his eyes like it hurts him to meet mine. "I didn't kiss you because I'm angry at you. I was pissed off at myself." His shoulders tense and bunch as he pushes himself away from the desk. "FUCK!" he yells.

He paces back and forth in front of the desk before stopping in front of me again.

"From the minute I saw you sleeping in your car, I wanted you, Becca." Kade raises his eyes and locks on me. I feel trapped in the raw hunger I see stamped on his face. "You were so fucking beautiful. Then when you sassed me, challenged me? Well fuck, I wanted you even more. Being around you is like, hell…pop rocks."

He sees the confusion on my face. "You remember holding pop rocks in your mouth when you were a kid? The way they would jump around, whizzing and popping off your tongue? My whole body feels like that when I'm around you."

Now I can't meet his eyes. I don't want him to see how hurt I am by his words.

"Bullshit Kade. You ignored me. After that first day, you didn't touch me or talk to me. You left the fucking room when I walked in." I try, but I can't hide the hurt in my voice. "You hugged me, you were treating me like someone that mattered, and then you just…turned your back on me like I was nothing." I rub my hands up and down my arms, feeling the same chill I felt the night he walked away from my apartment.

"You scare the hell out of me, Becca."

My eyes flip to his in disbelief. I search his gaze, looking for lies, but don't find them. Kade's gaze is holding mine, shadows dancing in his eyes.

"I have a type, Becca."

This is not something I want to hear. I don't want to know about other women and how I'm exactly like them. But my curiosity gets the better of me, keeping me from walking away from this conversation. Kade pauses, before pushing the words out, those painful, humiliating words.

Those words break me a little.

"The more broken a woman is, the more I want to be with her."

Snap. Another thread pulling me toward him breaks.

If I let him keep talking, there won't be any threads left drawing me to this man. Nothing that will pull me back to him. A mixture of anger and embarrassment colors my face. I clench my teeth, holding back the string of curses I want to throw at him. Who the hell does he think he is? I'm not some broken toy that needs fixing.

"My last girlfriend was an addict who stole from this shop. The one before that had a drinking problem. The one before that would pop pills, cheat on me, and then be so sorry I'd take her back. I wanted to help them all, fix them all. I always want to fix them."

Right. That's completely humiliating. Time for me to get the hell out of here.

"Got it. Well, you did a good job, Kade." The bitterness in my voice cut through the room. "You fixed me right up. Gave me a job, a place to stay. Give yourself a pat on the back." I take a deep breath, sucking back the flurry of angry words I want to shoot at him. "Now, I'm done with this conversation."

I give zero fucks about his feelings anymore. I'm out of here. Turning on my heel, I head toward the door into the shop, but Kade's voice freezes my feet before I can push through it.

"I did CPR on my mom three times before I was nine."

Jesus.

I shift my head, wanting, no, needing, to see him. His mouth is a tight slash, his eyebrows lowered over his eyes.

"She was an equal opportunity addict. If it would get her high, she'd fucking do it. Crack, Heroin, Meth. She did them all at one point or another. I don't remember her ever being sober, but until I was six or seven, she mostly held it together." His breath is sawing in and out of his chest, his face white. "We had a little apartment, and most of the time, we had food in the house. I could make mac and cheese on the stove by myself when I was five. Sandwiches even earlier. I'd feed my mom and then finish up whatever food was left."

I don't think there's anything he can say to change things, but I can't walk away in the face of his pain. I won't be that kind of person. "You were just a baby," I whisper, hurting for the little boy forced to grow up too soon.

Kade shakes his head, "I was the man of the house, Becca. I would clean up her puke and tuck her in bed. I'd sit with her to make sure she didn't stop breathing. It was my job to take care of her and keep her safe."

"No one helped you? A teacher, a social worker? Somebody?"

Kade's smile makes me feel young, naïve. "Sure, someone would call social services, and I'd get sent off to a foster home. But I always made my way back to my mom. She was all I had. She was the devil I knew."

His eyes drift away. "God, she was so beautiful. She lit up the room when she was happy. Fuck, most of the time, she was high as a kite, but it was easy to get caught up in her pull. She'd suck me in with her light, and then I'd be left in the dark when she crashed. It became this predictable, horrible pattern. I'd fix her up, then she'd fall apart, and I'd do it all over again."

"That's not okay, Kade."

"No Becca, it's not. But it was my life. Most of the kids in my apartment complex had it just as bad, if not worse."

"Worse? Worse than a Mom overdosing in front of you?"

Kade shifts his gaze into the garage, tracking Micah, who'd moved closer to help one of the other mechanics. "Micah had it so much worse." He says, sadness coating his words.

"Micah? Someone hurt him, didn't they?" The idea of parents hurting their own children enrages me, but that these two powerful men, men I respected, were hurt? My feelings were past rage and heading well into nuclear.

Kade's eyes are traveling over my face. "Yea, Micah's dad liked to beat on him. He beat him so badly once he ended up in the hospital." He hesitates before adding, "He suffered permanent brain damage."

My hands fly to my mouth to cover my sob, heart hurting for that little boy, and for the man I consider a friend. "His speech!"

Kade nods slowly. "His speech. The language center of his brain was damaged. It makes it hard for him to put together sentences, especially if he's stressed or around new people. He's so fucking smart, Becca, but he can't get the words out."

"Tell me where his father is now." My voice is ice cold.

Kade's eyes are hard as they meet mine. "He's been dealt with."

"Where is he, Kade?" I push. I want to find him. I want to break him. I have so many ideas. So many skills. I could make the pain last for days, all without drawing blood.

"He's dead, Becca." Those eyes of his are still hard.

My anger dulls a little, but I still need to know. "Did it hurt?"

Kade's smile would be chilling if I wasn't perfect ready to kill Micah's father myself. "Yes, Becca. It did."

That makes me feel a little better. "Good. That piece of shit should be rotting."

His smile shifts, warms. "You're a bloodthirsty woman, Becca. I like it."

My glare only makes his smile grow. That smile kills me. It starts to knit those snapped threads. I can't allow that. This man is attracted to me because he met me at my lowest point. He looked at me, and his programming wouldn't let him walk away.

My sadness over the life he was forced to lead softens my voice.

"Kade. Thank you for sharing all of that with me. It helps. And it's okay. I understand why you backed off. We're okay."

"What do you understand, Becca?" Kade asks evenly.

I sigh, releasing the last of my anger. Letting all the foolish hope I had built around this man drift away with it. "I understand that you looked at me and saw someone who needed fixing." I shrug. "I appreciate it, Kade. I do. I was in a not very good spot. My shitty situation met your fucked up past, and you couldn't do anything but help. I'm grateful. But me sticking around any longer is not good for either of us."

Kade nods slowly. "Maybe at first, that was true. Helping the girl. Trying to fix her is a pretty solid pattern in my life. More than one of my brothers has pointed that out to me."

My eyes widen. "Brothers? You've only ever mentioned one."

Kade laughs softly. "They're not blood brothers, Becca. They're more than that." Kade pauses, smiling softly, his eyes drifting to the past. "My last time in state care, I ended up in a group home. It was a pretty shitty place. My mom had died a few years before, and Micah and I had run pretty wild. Doing whatever we had to do to stay out of the system and, in Micah's case, away from his dad. When they finally caught up with us, and they couldn't pin any of the shit we'd done on us, they stuck us in the home together. That's where Ransom found us all. He was bigger, older, and he made us a family." His smile shifts into a smirk. "Well, a gang at first, then a family. We called ourselves the Brash Brothers."

I raise my eyebrow. "The Brash Brothers?"

Kade laughs. "Yea, I know. One counselor at the group home called Ransom brash. It wasn't a compliment, but Ran liked it, and it stuck. Fuck, half of us didn't even know what it meant, but we thought it sounded cool."

"And you're still in each other's lives?" I asked.

"Yep. We built Brash Auto together. This was our first garage. I'm still not sure how Ransom got his hands on it, but we did whatever we had to do to make it a success. We've got a ton of them now, with another dozen set to open this year." He shrugs. "Ransom's got us in a bunch of other stuff, but I don't really handle that part of the business."

This piece of him, the way he talks about his family, leaves me a mix of happy and sad. Happy that he has family, people he clearly loves. But it emphasizes how truly alone I am now. Dad and I were such a great team. I never felt like I needed anyone else. Losing him felt like losing a limb. I have to learn how to walk again.

"So, you run this garage for him?" I've barely seen him, and something tells me he's got a lot more going on.

He smiles and shrugs again. "I'm the Chief Operating Officer. I oversee all the garages."

13

KADE

"Why the hell were you doing all this then?" She asks, waving her arm around the office. I can't help but smile at the disbelief on her face and in her voice. It's cleared away the anger from before. I'm so fucking relieved she's actually talking to me again. I couldn't let her just walk out of my life.

"This place feels like home," I admit to her. "That apartment you're staying in? That was the first home I felt completely safe in. This garage? We built this garage, Becca. A bunch of reject kids did this. We were told over and over we were useless, a fucking drain on society. That we weren't going to amount to anything. But we proved them wrong. This place was ours."

I breathe in the familiar smell of oil and exhaust overlaid with the smell of lemon. Over all of it, I still smell her. Christ, her scent is so deep in me by now that I could find that mix of vanilla and mint in the middle of a hurricane. I rub the back of my neck, shifting to relieve the tension and bring myself back to the conversation.

"I'm having a hard time letting it go," I admit. "And

Micah, well, I don't think there's any way he'll leave. I need to be here for him."

Becca's studying me. Assessing. "But do you, though?"

My body stills. "What the fuck do you mean?"

Her sharp eyes cut through me. "You've barely been here the last three weeks. Micah and I have been communicating just fine. He passes me notes like back in high school. We text. I've been learning some signs. It's kinda fun."

She's smiling, and I push away a spurt of jealousy at the affection in her voice when she talks about Micah. I should be happy Micah's doing okay. I am happy. But she doesn't look at me like that. And I know it's my own fucking fault.

"He interacts with the guys, Kade. He's always ready to lend a hand. The other guys look up to him. They respect him."

I shift my eyes over to the garage, finding Micah in bay three. He's working with Jamie, one of the junior mechanics. As I watch, he smiles and nods, patting Jamie on the back. Jamie is asking questions, getting nods or shakes of the head from Micah. Micah looks…confident.

When did that happen? How did I not notice when Micah stopped being that angry teenager? The one that would fight to get his words out, then use his fists instead to make his point? Becca's eyes are soft and far too knowing.

"You're a caretaker, Kade. You collect people. You said yourself. You want to fix people." Her smile is understanding. The idea that she might see me clearly is unsettling. "You're good at it." She continues, "Maybe you did your job with Micah but didn't notice?"

"Maybe," I admit, uncomfortable with how much I missed with Micah. He's apparently a pretty big fucking blind spot.

"Micah is stronger than you think, Kade. Talk with him about what's going on. He might surprise you."

I nod. Fuck. Maybe that conversation is way overdue, but it'll keep a little longer. Right now, Becca's in front of me, and

I can see on her face that she's still leaving. I need her to stay more than I need my next breath.

"Would you stay, Becca? Please? I'd really like it if we could start over." I'm not ashamed to beg. "I can't get you out of my system, and I really don't want to keep trying."

Becca gives me a sad smile that makes my stomach churn. "I don't think so, Kade. I don't need you to fix me. This dynamic is not healthy."

"Fuck Becca, I already know you don't need me fixing you," I snap, frustrated. I stop, not really wanting to explain how I know that, but I don't have anything left to lose at this point.

"I kept looking for your screwups," I admit, feeling pretty fucking stupid. "I'd check the books at night. I'd double-check the parts orders. Hell, I even did inventory counts. I tried to figure out all the ways you could steal from me. And I didn't find anything." I push my hands through my hair, afraid to look at her. "Of course I didn't find anything. Because you're completely unlike any woman I've ever been with."

I risk a glance at her face. She looks pissed, but not more pissed than before. Fuck. Time to go all in.

"Becca. I really didn't want to find anything bad, and I settled down after the first week. But I kept coming back to see you. It fucking killed me to see your face light up for the guys and the customers and then go blank when you look at me. I want your sun shining on me, Becca. Please."

I pause, trying to gauge her reaction, but she's giving me nothing. I am such an asshole. Her choice shouldn't be between staying and being with me, or leaving. I feel my chest deflate.

"Stay, please. You don't have to leave, and…I'll stay away if you want me to. I swear it. It'll fucking kill me, but I'll do it."

She blows out a frustrated breath. "You're so damn

confusing, Kade." She throws her arms out in frustration. "Can you just be straight with me for once! What do you WANT?"

I lock my eyes on her. "I want you under me, begging me to go deeper, harder. I want your nails digging into my back and your pussy wrapped around me."

Her eyes widen, and she retreats a step. Fuck, maybe I shouldn't have been quite so honest.

14

BECCA

Holy crap.

This man is scorching. The way he's looking at me makes my girl parts happy. My chest feels hot, and I know I'll be blushing in a minute. I was not expecting that. I feel slightly less pathetic, realizing the attraction definitely goes both ways. I get lost picturing the two of us together. Wondering how it would feel to have Kade's powerful body between my thighs. His voice startles me out of my imagination.

"What do you want, Bec?"

Crap. What do I want? This morning I thought I knew what I wanted. To leave. To make a new home at the Dojo, make some friends, and feel like myself again.

This time at the garage, obsessing over Kade, felt like a break from my life. But spending all this time here with the guys made me realize that I desperately miss the Dojo. I miss the students and instructors. I miss feeling part of the team. I feel like I belong there in a way I just don't here.

"I don't want to work here anymore, Kade," I admit. "I'm so grateful for the work, and I'm so glad I could help you. But I want to work at the Dojo."

The resignation on his face I expect, but the determination that swiftly follows surprises me. "Don't work here then. But what about us?"

"I...uh, I'm feeling a bit lost here, Kade," I admit, scratching my fingers through my hair and looking at the floor.

He pushes. "It's a simple question, Becca. Do you want me?"

Agh!

"It's not a simple question, Kade! Do I want to fuck you? Yea, I'd like to climb you like a tree, maybe sit on your face. But it's not that simple!"

Kade smiles and starts to walk around the desk.

"FREEZE!" I yell at him, startling him to a stop. He looks at me in puzzlement.

"Look, I'm sorry I'm having a bit of trouble adjusting to your complete one-eighty right now. This morning you were avoiding me, and now you want...what? To fuck like bunnies? Then what?"

Kade exhales, then slides his hands into the pockets of his pants, making the fabric pull against his groin. I gulp a little at the bulge and flip my eyes to the ceiling for a minute.

"That's up to you," he mumbles.

I arch an eyebrow at him and cross my arms over my chest. "Suddenly I have a say?"

He winces, then exhales again before meeting my eyes and completely blowing my mind.

"Yea Becca. It's clear I didn't do a good job showing you. But the truth is, I'm fucking obsessed with you. I fought it for a while, but I'd be happier sitting all night on your doorstep than fucking anybody else." He clasps his hands at the back of his neck, looking down at his feet before meeting my eyes again. "I didn't see you coming. And now, well, you can do anything you want with me. But please, for fuck's sake, give me a chance."

I gulp, drowning in the sincerity in his voice and gaze. "A chance?" I rasp.

He nods, "I'll take anything, Becca. Any speed you want to go, I'm with you. Fuck I'll walk you to and from work. I'll carry your fucking purse. I mean it. ANYTHING." His eyes are burning, and his face is tense. He looks like he's in pain. And I'm reeling. I search his eyes again, but all I see is truth and want.

This man.

This beautiful, broken, successful man wants me.

All the feelings I've been pushing down rise in me again. The possibilities stretch out before me. He's shared more of himself today than I could have hoped for. But in the back of my mind is a niggling worry. Worry that this is fleeting. Worry that he'll change his mind. Worry that he's still somehow confusing his feelings for me with his need to help me. To fix me.

I don't need a hero.

But I do want a partner. A ride or die. Can this man give me that? He seems to have no problem giving away his money or his time. Can he love me the way I deserve to be loved?

And there I go, getting way ahead of myself.

We haven't even been on a date. This could all crash and burn tomorrow.

But so what? I've crashed and burned before. And I've come back from it. I could do it again if I had to.

I straighten my spine as clarity comes to me. I can't control what he does or how he feels. But if he's telling the truth about his feelings, I know I want to explore it. I would regret it for the rest of my life if I didn't.

"Kade," I say firmly, "I'm taking the job at the Dojo, and I'll help you find someone to replace me here. Then I'll quit." I take a deep breath, studying his pained face. "Until then, you're still my boss." I raise my hand, stopping his objections. "I'm okay with dating the boss, though," I say with a smile.

His body settles, and a sexy grin curls the corners of his mouth.

"We date. You can pick me up after work. We spend time together. And once I'm not your employee anymore, if things are still good…then I'll sit on your face." I nod, pleased with my plan.

Kade's big smile and low chuckle make my heart stutter. Crap. I need to change my underwear. And buy a new vibrator. It's going to be a long couple of weeks.

15

BECCA

How exactly does one prepare for a first date with your boss? It was a mistake to Google it. I ended up in a death spiral of porn video ads and had to abandon my laptop. Why the fuck would people want to play a cartoon sex video game, anyway?

People are fucking strange.

"Crap," I mutter, catching the time on my phone. He's going to be here any minute, and I'm still in the same pink T-shirt and camo leggings I wore at work today. Maybe I should put in a bit more of an effort, but Kade's already seen me in this today. I should be trying to pretty it up. Put my best foot forward and all that. But I don't see the point. This is the type of outfit I live in. I don't see that changing anytime soon. Plus, Kade was going to bring dinner here.

I'm stupidly excited to spend time with him. The tension of the last few weeks is finally broken. Now the hard work begins. Seeing if we actually like each other outside of the office. I know what it's like to be attracted to someone you work closely with.

That's how I ended up with my first boyfriend. And my third. They were both black belt students at the Dojo, and we spent a ton of time together. My first boyfriend, Josh, was a tall, gangly guy, and I was completely obsessed. We dated for an entire month. He ended up breaking up with me because he said he wanted to date a girl that couldn't beat him up.

It sucked.

And for a long time, it made me wonder if I'd have to make myself smaller, both in body and personality, to get a guy.

I dated someone outside of the Dojo for a while before my third boyfriend, Matt. He was different. He loved how tough I was, and I loved how kind he was. Our relationship was comfortable, but when he went away to school, we drifted apart, proximity being the core of our relationship.

Even in our most intimate moments, no boyfriend has made me feel the way I feel when Kade's just standing next to me. Like I'm totally and completely alive.

The knock on the door sets my heart racing. I take a deep breath, open the door and look my fill at him. He changed out of his dress pants into faded jeans and a plain black T-shirt. My eyes trace over the tattoos peeking out from his sleeves. I can't decide which version of Kade I like best. The businessman or the mechanic.

Good thing I don't have to choose.

I skim my eyes back up, landing on Kade's face. His eyebrow is arched, and he's smirking. I smile, not even a little embarrassed to be caught.

"You can't blame a girl for looking," I say. He laughs that same rusty-sounding laugh from this afternoon. It always sounds like he's out of practice. I wonder why? He seems to have everything going for him. Money, work, friends. Other than once or twice with Micah, and early on with me, I've never seen him really relaxed and laughing.

"Can I come in?"

"Right! Crap. Come in." I step back and hold the door open for him. He steps in, stopping right next to me.

He gently pushes the door closed, locks it, then turns those dark eyes on me. I watch him through my lashes as he slowly lowers his head to me, brushing his freshly shaven cheek against mine before pressing the softest, most gentle kiss to the corner of my mouth. My whole body shivers, and I stutter out a breath. I feel his smile against my skin before he pulls back. I think I even mutter something super sophisticated like "Woah."

I briefly wish that I was someone who could play it cool. But I'm not. I never will be. If losing Dad taught me anything, it's that life is too short to play games. Kade's going to know exactly where he stands with me because I just don't want to do this any other way.

I reach up and rub my fingers over his smooth cheek. His eyes close, and he tilts into my hand, his big chest deflating with his exhale. I like that this attraction goes both ways. But I'm in big trouble if this keeps up. We're thirty seconds into this date, and I already want to see what other reactions I can get from him.

My cheeks flush as I imagine having him spread out under me, letting me touch and explore his powerful body. I want to know what spots make him moan and which ones make him lose control. I give his cheek a little scratch with my fingernails.

"Take your shoes off."

He raises his brow again but toes off his boots without complaint, leaving him in plain black socks. He lines them up neatly next to mine. His shoes look massive next to my size elevens, and it makes me smile. I move into the kitchen on my bare feet.

"Can I get you a drink? I grabbed some beer and pop at the store."

Kade's eyebrows arrow down. "I didn't think about…how are you getting to the store?"

"I took the bus a couple of times." His growl interrupts

me, and I shoot him a dirty look before continuing, "Micah lent me his car twice too."

"I don't like that you're taking the bus," he admits, rubbing the back of his neck.

"Lots of people take the bus, Kade. The stop's not that far. It's not a big deal."

"Let me get your car—"

"Nope. We're not discussing the car. When I have the money to fix it, then we'll talk."

He pushes his hands through his hair in frustration. "Promise me you'll let me drive you next time?"

"No, but I'll ask you for a ride if I need one." I smile and wink at him to soften my words. He grumbles and scowls. But that's all he's going to get out of me. I've seen how much the man works. How busy he is. There's no reason for him to chauffeur me around.

Plus, this is too new, and I don't want to be that dependent on him for anything right now. Everything changed this afternoon, but I don't think I trust him to not turn back into the reserved guy who ignored me for weeks.

"So," I say, ready to change the subject, "weren't you bringing dinner." Kade's face reddens slightly, and it's freaking adorable. He threads his fingers through the back of his hair, and I'm immediately distracted by watching the muscles in his bicep shift.

"I uh…realized I didn't actually ask you what you wanted. I thought maybe we could pick something out together, and I'll run and grab it. Or we could go out?" He looks at me expectantly. Right. Stop staring and talk to the man.

"My socks are off, Kade."

"Ah…I see that." He pauses, confused. "You said it like I should know what that means."

"I have to wear closed-toed shoes in the garage, Kade. I

hate shoes. My feet must be free. I'm not putting shoes back on today."

He's chuckling again. "Okay. So we eat here. Wouldn't want to cage the toes again."

Jeez, I like him. He couldn't give me shit about the shoe thing, but he seems happy to roll with whatever. But I'm really freaking hungry, so I head to the fridge and start pulling out ingredients.

"Becca…what are you doing?" he asks in confusion.

"Getting taco stuff out. I'm starving."

"Fuck." The sorry in his voice pulls my head out of the fridge. "I'll go grab something quick. I can be back in twenty."

My heart drops…this is so bad. "You…you," I can't even get the words out, even the idea of it so horrible. "You don't like tacos?" I'm horrified. I'm sure my face is a combination of *who the fuck are you* and *get out of my house*.

Kade's booming laughter suddenly fills the small room. "Fuck, Becca. The look on your face." He snorts and wipes his eyes. "I just meant that I asked you on a date. It's my job to feed you."

I nod but push for clarification. "But how do you feel about tacos?" I cross my arms.

He studies me before huffing out another laugh. "I fucking love tacos."

I relax, glad one of the biggest relationship hurdles we've ever faced in our five minutes of dating has been jumped over.

"That could have been a deal-breaker, dude." I smile like I'm joking. But I'm really not. Kade's really hot. But…Tacos. He's shaking his head at me, but it's okay. He can think I'm ridiculous as long as he keeps looking at me with those warm eyes of his.

"You're…going to cook me dinner? Like from scratch?" He sounds surprised, and I can't decide if I should be offended that he doubts my skills or sad that no one's cooked for him. I settled for snorting and shaking my head.

"No way," I say, seeing his smile dim slightly. "You're helping. Grab a knife and a cutting board and get your ass over here."

His smile comes back in full force as he follows my instructions. It stays as he methodically cuts the veggies. We work side by side at the counter, arms brushing and assembling our dinner. We settle into the small two-seater table loaded with bowls of meat and toppings.

Kade groans when he takes his first bite, then quickly takes another. I hum in agreement, my mouth too stuffed to talk. So. Good. When the edge is taken off our hunger, we settle back in our chairs.

"You know, this is the best meal I've ever eaten from this kitchen." He says, his eyes drifting across the food left on the table.

"Really? Didn't you live here for a while? You guys must have cooked, right?" Kade slouches down in his chair, stretching his legs out on either side of mine.

"Oh, we cooked. We couldn't afford not to. We ate way too much spaghetti with plain tomato sauce…I haven't had spaghetti since we moved out." His lips turn down, and he shudders at the memory. "I think we lived here a year before we bought a salt shaker. Everything was bland or burnt. No, in between."

"Who did the cooking?" I'm so curious about these boys who made themselves into a family. The sheer will it must have taken to pull them together and keep them together is astonishing.

"Ransom at first. But he was the oldest, so he was the one out front most of the time. The rest of us took turns. Except Jonas. He'd spend the entire night trying to find just the right recipe, and if he did, it took him a fucking hour to cut the onion up into perfectly even pieces. We'd have ended up so hungry we would've stuffed ourselves with shitty sand-wiches instead."

Every time he talks about his brothers, his voice softens, his love for them coming through clearly. I can picture them all here, groaning about how hungry they are and picking on each other. It sounds busy and crowded.

It sounds like family.

"I always wished I had siblings," I say. "What was it like, all of you living together?"

"It was a fucking madhouse." His grin widens. "We were complete savages most of the time. There was a fight almost daily when we lived here."

"You guys seriously all lived in this place? How? How on earth does that work?"

"Not very well. It was wall-to-wall sleeping bags in here. We were supposed to age out of the group home, but none of us stayed that long before getting the fuck out. We'd land here and Ransom just kept buying sleeping bags."

"No one came looking for you?"

He scoffs and shakes his head. "They didn't give a shit we weren't there. As long as we didn't get arrested, we could stay off the children's services radar. It helped that we were all big."

"All big? Like you and Micah? You know you guys are outside the curve, right?"

He smirks. "In every way."

My face flushes, and I throw my wadded-up napkin at him. He laughs as it bounces off his chest.

"Most of us are big, yeah. I think that's how Ransom picked us at first. He was building a gang, and having big guys is a fucking requirement. Jonas and Zach are a bit smaller, but they had other things going for them."

"He sounds very calculated," I say, wondering why he would go to all that trouble. You think it would have been easier for him to stay on his own, only worrying about himself. But clearly, his gamble paid off.

"He was. He is. I can't say that I understand fully why he did it either. Or that he knew we'd be as successful as we are. But I'm pretty fucking grateful that he picked me."

"You love him a lot," I say. He leans forward and crosses his arms on the table, his eyes studying the wall next to the fridge. I noticed it when I moved in. How could I not? I mean, most apartments don't have a graffiti wall. I'd studied it a bit and found all the names hidden within the stylized word BRASH.

"Love? Yeah. But it's more than that. I owe him my life. I respect the hell out of him, and I would walk through fucking fire for him."

I can see all of that on his face. He's been so removed the last few weeks, so I soak in the play of emotions on his face. He's letting me see the way he feels about his brothers. He is capable of such deep emotion. Such deep love. The men that inspired that must be pretty amazing.

I've met families that ignored each other. That put each other down. They tarnish the word family. But Kade and his brothers? They sound like everything a family should be. Who gives a damn if they're not blood?

"What's wrong?" His question pulls me out of my thoughts.

"I'm jealous of you." I wince as I say it, but there it is. Kade scowls and sits back in his chair.

"Jealous?" His laugh is harsh. "Why the fuck would you ever feel jealous of me?"

"Seriously?" Does he really not see it? His eyes narrow, and he stares at me. "Kade. When you met me, I was sleeping in my car. I had a cellphone full of acquaintances. Nobody I know who would drop everything and come and help me. Nobody." I pause, letting that sink in. "If something bad had happened to me, the hospital wouldn't have had anyone to call. You," I say, pointing right at his oblivious face, "would have a waiting room full of men who love you. You would never be alone. That's a pretty special thing." He takes a deep breath and crosses his arms loosely over his chest.

"I hadn't really thought of it that way," he says, looking embarrassed.

"Well, you should. You have something not everybody does. I get you had a hard childhood, but look what you have now," I say, gesturing to the graffiti wall. His eyes warm as they travel over the wall.

"You're right," he says quietly.

"I know. I always am. It's a curse," I tease, wanting to break the tension. Kade laughs but leans forward again, locking his intense eyes on me.

"Becca," he says, his voice more serious than I've ever heard it. "It's me. You call me. Do it right now." I raise my eyebrows in confusion. "Get your phone out and set me as your emergency contact."

I study his face, looking for…I don't know what. All I see is certainty. I rise slowly, getting my phone off the counter and sitting back down. I'm conscious of his intense gaze on me. I avoid his eyes as I open up his contact. My finger hovers over the *Add to Emergency Contact* field. I look up at him, torn.

"Do it, Becca. Just the fucking idea of you being hurt and me not knowing about it is making me insane. I need this. Please," he pleads.

Somehow, this feels like jumping off a cliff.

"I…I don't know."

He frowns, his arms tensing. "What is there to think about?" I could tread lightly here. Soften my words, pretty them up.

But I won't.

"You run a little hot and cold," I tell him truthfully. "I don't know that I can trust you to be there if something bad happens."

He freezes, and even though he tries to hide it, I can see the hurt on his face.

"I think you're a good guy, Kade. There's a lot about you to like. That's why we're sitting here right now. And I know you had your reasons for keeping your distance. I just…you walked away."

He laughs, but there's no humor in the sound. "I told you a bit about my relationships," he says, exhaling heavily. I nod, and he continues, "I'm always the guy you call. Left rehab early and keyed a cop car? Call Kade. Cheated on me with another guy who kicks you out in the middle of the night? Call Kade. This is fucking ironic." He pauses, rubbing his eyebrow.

"I'm always the guy that's there. No matter how much I was hurt or how shitty things were. I always showed up. So when I met you, I…I was so fucking drawn to you. Everything was so much bigger than I'd ever felt before that I panicked a bit. I did the opposite of what I normally do. I stayed away."

I smile sadly, watching him carefully. I honestly don't understand how a woman could treat her boyfriend that way.

And I really don't understand why he'd allow it.

He rises, sliding me out, chair and all, from the table so he can crouch in front of me. He puts his calloused hands on my knees, gripping tightly. He looks so solid. Immovable.

"I will show up for you, Becca. You have my word." The sincerity in his voice sinks through my doubts. It's so tempting to believe him.

"And what if we don't work out?" I ask softly, looking down at him.

Kade's mouth tightens. "It doesn't matter. As long as you need me, I'm there, Becca. I swear it."

I see the truth of it in his eyes. He means every word. Can I let the last three weeks go? Can I move forward, giving him the trust he seems to need? I lean into him, running my fingers over the frown lines in his forehead, then down over the bridge of his nose. His eyes close, and he exhales heavily. He reaches up and takes my hand in his, pressing his lips softly to my palm. The devotion, the promise in that kiss, is like nothing I've ever experienced.

I jump.

I push *Add to Emergency Contacts,* then drop my phone with a clatter. I spread my thighs, reaching up to pull him into me by the back of his neck. He buries his face in my neck, his hot breath fanning against me, his arms sliding behind my back. My hand, still held tightly in his, now pressed against his cheek.

"Okay," I whisper.

16

BECCA

My hands are shaking as I smooth down my red flowing dress. Kade doesn't seem to care what I'm wearing, but I wanted a change from the leggings and T-shirts. I'm wearing an actual bra for this date. Not one of my familiar sports bras. Tonight, I want to feel like a sexy, attractive woman.

We've been spending almost every night together for the last week, but it's always been here. We'll make dinner, watch movies, chat, and it's been amazing. But Kade insisted we go on a proper date, and I'm stupidly nervous. I know how to be the tomboy, the girl-friend in a group of guys.

Hell, most of the guys I've dated in the past I knew my whole life. There was no mystery. No surprises. Kade's different. We're different. He's been more open than before. It's clear he's trying. But there's so much I don't know about him.

Every night I'm surprised by some new piece of information. But he doesn't really volunteer anything from his past until I ask. Our conversations flow so naturally on almost every other topic, but the past? Nah, not happening.

Kade's soft knock sets off the butterflies, and I take a few deep breaths to calm myself. I know I've hit the mark with my choice of outfit when I open the door and his eyes flare, mouth dropping open.

"Holy Fuck," he mutters, unable to tear his eyes away from me. They travel along my body, snagging on the low V-neck before darting away to my bare arms, then the flirty hem flirting with the skin above my knee. He examines me like he doesn't want to miss anything.

I feel the blush rising in my chest. I have to resist the urge to fidget or make a stupid joke. That's what I always do when I'm uncomfortable, but tonight I'm going to sit with the discomfort. Because I like this man's eyes on me. I like that I feel beautiful and desirable when he looks at me. So I won't make a joke and break the tension.

I'm going to revel in it instead.

Kade's glittering eyes finally meet mine, and he swallows deeply. "You look so fucking beautiful, Becca."

Jesus, I feel my nipples harden and pray that my padded bra hides the reaction. I don't really mind him knowing how he affects me, but I don't want a whole restaurant looking at my nips. I lick my dry lips.

"Thank you. You look amazing, too." He's so sexy. Wearing a dark, fitted suit, his crisp white shirt makes his skin look golden in the dim light of the apartment. The collar is open, and I have to smile

"No tie?"

Kade shakes his head. "I can't stand 'em. I used to try, back when we started expanding, but I was so distracted by the fucking thing I couldn't focus."

"Do any of your brothers wear a tie?" I'm deeply curious about where he goes and the people he spends his days with. I want to know more about his brothers.

His smile crinkles up the corner of his eyes. "Some," he shrugs. "Ransom does sometimes. A few of the other guys do too, depending on the situation. But Jonas has a thing about clothes. He only dresses in things he feels are comfortable.

The fucking president could come to visit, and he'd still wear a T-shirt and cardigan."

I laugh and slide my feet into my heels, Kade's hand on my elbow to stabilize me. I don't need help to balance, but no way am I telling him that. I just enjoy the feel of his hand on me instead.

"What does Jonas do again?" I can't remember which brother he is.

"He's the money guy. CFO technically. All I know is if it involves numbers, he's the guy to talk to."

The awe in Kade's voice is interesting. He doesn't talk about anyone in quite the same way, not even Ransom.

"You respect him," I say.

Kade nods and escorts me down the stairs and through the yard to his truck. I'm on the verge of asking more questions when he speaks again.

"Jonas is like no one I've ever met." Kade opens the door and waits for me to settle in the seat before continuing. "He's got Autism. I don't really know the specifics. Jonas doesn't really talk about it. But the way his brain works is fucking magical." He closes the door and jogs around, hopping into the driver's seat of the truck.

"Magical?"

Kade smiles as he starts the truck. "He remembers fucking everything," he laughs before clarifying. "Well, when it comes to numbers, anyway. He couldn't tell you what he ordered for lunch today at a restaurant, but he'll remember how much every item on the bill was."

I smile, completely fascinated. "He sounds unique."

Kade shrugs. "He's my brother."

The easy way he says that. The absolute confidence he has in their relationship steals my breath for a moment. I rub my aching chest.

"You okay?" Kade asks with a frown.

"Yeah, I'm good."

Kade shoots me a look, but he lets it go and we sit listening to the quiet radio, watching the setting sun light up the high-rises around us, lost in our own thoughts.

I'm not okay.

I'm alone.

I love hearing about all of Kade's brothers. If Kade and Micah's relationship is typical of the way they all interact, then they love each other, flaws and all. They're this battle-worn and scarred unit.

Perfect in its imperfection.

And I want that with every cell in my body. I want to have a home. I want people I know I can depend on when life gets stormy. People who are there to hold me up when I need it. And who know without a shadow of a doubt that I'll be there for them too, no questions asked.

I had that with Dad. And while he was alive, I thought I had it with the family we built at the Dojo. But the ties that bound us were weak, unable to take the death and grief that wore away at them like acid.

But Kade's family? They were forged in fire, in hardship, the connections between them made of the strongest steel. Unbreakable. I wonder, not for the first time, if there's room for a new member.

"THIS IS THE FANCIEST RESTAURANT I'VE EVER BEEN TO," I whisper to Kade as we follow the waitress through the dimly lit room, my fingers tangled with his. I swear thousands of little chandeliers light the way, their crystals reflecting the candles at each table. I worry again that I'm underdressed. Wishing for a moment that I was small and delicate and could flow through a room, easily weaving through tables.

But then I'd have to give up my stellar ass. That would be sad, so maybe I'm better off with the big ass and wide hips. They've served me well up to this point.

I return my focus to the room and the hostess' swinging hips. She nearly smacks an older gentleman's elbow as she passes. I'd wonder what Kade's thinking of her ass if he wasn't gently stroking my thumb as we walk.

He's not thinking of her at all.

When we get to the table, Kade pulls out my chair. I have a moment of panic, wondering how the hell that works, then decide to hover like I'm using the grungy bathroom at the beach I used to go to as a kid. It works, and I relax and sit when I feel the chair sliding in.

My fingers tap the underside of the table nervously as the hostess leaves, and the waitress takes our drink orders. I feel completely out of place. But not Kade. No, he looks like he eats here every night. How does this man go from hands covered in grease to wearing a... "How much did your suit cost?"

Kade's mouth twitches, his eyes twinkling at me. "You sound a little riled up there, Bec. Do you not like my suit?"

I narrow my eyes at him. "You're dodging the question. How much did it cost?"

Kade's smile dims, and he shrugs, "A few grand, I think. "

"Right," I mutter as I look down at my thirty dollar Target dress.

"Becca," Kade says softly, "look at me." Though his tone is soft, I hear the steel in his words. I reluctantly raise my eyes to meet his. I swallow thickly.

"I don't fit in here, Kade."

His eyes sharpen on mine, and his forehead creases. "The fuck you don't."

I tighten my lips. "My menu doesn't have any prices on it, but I'm pretty sure a salad will cost more than I paid for my dress." I shift my gaze around the room. "No other woman in here is wearing something from Target." Jesus, I want to punch myself in the tit for the words coming out of my mouth. But I am so out of my comfort zone here.

"I don't give a fuck what any other woman is wearing. You're the only person in this place I care about, Becca." Kade's eyes are hard, glittering. I touch the top of his clenched hand, and he flips it to wrap my hand in his.

"I know," I whisper, "but…" I search for the words to explain to him what I'm feeling. "Most of my life has been spent in sweats. I can count on one hand the number of times I've worn a dress in the last five years. I just…" My words drift off. I feel so stupid.

"You're not comfortable here," he says flatly.

I wish I could say yes. I'm fine. And just forget about what I'm feeling. But I'm not about to start lying to him. "You fit, Kade. I don't. No, I'm not comfortable," I admit.

Kade's snort makes my eyes widen. "You fit in here a fuck of a lot more than I do, Becca." I don't like that tone in his voice. He sounds…self-deprecating.

"From over here, you look like you fit in perfectly."

He shakes his head. "I've eaten out of a fucking dumpster, Becca. I've slept under overpasses and used my fists to take what I needed. This is not my fucking world. I just visit it when I have to."

"Have to…and you have to tonight?" I'm really confused now. "Why are we here, Kade?"

His hand tightens on mine as he shoves his other one through his hair. "I wanted to take you somewhere you deserved."

I tighten my fingers on his. "And I deserve this restaurant?" I ask, still confused.

"You deserve the best, Becca," he says with absolute sincerity.

I exhale, the air leaving me in a rush. I extend my other hand across the table in invitation. Kade takes it, his focus completely on me.

"I love that you think that. I really do. But do you like it here? The truth Kade."

He slowly shakes his head and mutters, "We've done a few deals here, but I hate it. I feel like I'm in a fucking fishbowl. It's the best restaurant in the city, and I don't get it. The portions are way too small, and I usually have to hit a drive-thru after."

I let out a giggle of relief. Kade's lips tilt, too. "Kade."

"Becca."

"I'm pretty sure I saw an Outback a couple blocks away. Can we go there? I'd really like a Bloomin' Onion."

Kade's smile grows, his eyes lighting up. "Fuck yeah we can. I'll take you anywhere you want."

Kade stands and throws a hundred-dollar bill on the table, then grabs my hand and rushes us out the door.

I laugh the whole way to Outback.

17

BECCA

Kade's laughter is such a turn-on. Maybe it's not just the laughter. It's the fact that I'm the one making him laugh that feels so good. He can be so contained. So serious. He takes so much on. Being able to help him lighten up feels important and makes me feel like I'm giving him something he can't get elsewhere.

Kade throws his hand up. "Wait...you're telling me you shit your pants in front of the entire class?" He's gasping for breath, his laughter choked. He's slouched down onto the bench, completely relaxed. His jacket and cufflinks discarded a few minutes into our meal, his sleeves rolled up those tanned forearms.

We're one of the last ones in the restaurant, our meals finished hours ago. Kade paid the bill and tipped so well the staff has been happy to let us sit, coming by to keep our waters filled but otherwise leaving us alone.

"Not just crapped, Kade. Dad had taken me for ice cream at lunch..." I sigh. "It just..." I make an exploding gesture with my hands, "splattered out. Into my white Gi."

Kade is howling now, tears running down his face. He's clutching his stomach. "Oh, fuck Becca. Holy fuck."

Time to finish him. "It got around the whole Dojo, Kade. Most of the kids called me Torpedo Butt until I was thirteen."

He's laughing so hard now that he's stopped making noise. His whole body convulses in the booth. I cover my mouth, snorting with him. It was horrifying as an eight-year-old, but now, decades later, I can see the humor in the whole thing. And you can be damn sure if it had happened to any of the boys, I would have made up a killer nickname for them too.

I watch as Kade slowly calms, running my eyes over his wide shoulders and sexy arms to the hands currently covering his face.

Finally, he sighs and rubs his eyes. "Fuck Becca. That's the funniest thing I've ever heard." I nod, putting on a serious face, unable to help myself.

"You should have *heard it* then," I say with wide eyes and an eyebrow wiggle.

And he's off.

When he finally settles down, he asks, "What did your dad do?"

I smile, remembering my dad's attempt at comforting me. "He wrapped a sweater around me, and he took me home to change. He kept telling me it'll be okay, everyone will forget, but he laughed the whole time. He snickered every time I got called Torpedo Butt." I pause, remembering. "Actually, I'm pretty sure he called me Torpedo Butt when he talked to other people, but he never did it to my face."

Kade laughs and whistles. "I bet that pissed you off."

"So much," I say, smiling. "But that's just who he was. He didn't baby me. He figured I might as well toughen up. So I learned to roll with the nickname. I can't say I ever loved it, but it stopped hurting me. Not getting a reaction out of me made it boring for them, maybe?"

I snicker. "Plus," I say, holding up a finger, "I got boobs, and the boys figured they might have a better shot at getting near them if they stopped calling me names."

"That would do it. Teen boys think of breasts more than anything else."

I raise my eyebrows. "Really? More than anything else? Even you?"

Kade snorts. "Me more than most. I spent all my time with eight other boys, Becca. We spent our nights either talking about boobs or measuring the size of our dicks."

It was my turn to laugh. God, picturing a bunch of hormonal boys hiding a ruler made my eyes water.

"Oh Jesus, Kade, tell me you guys had a notebook to keep track of dick growth."

"Yep. It had a page for each of us. I'm happy to report we're all doing quite well in that department."

I feel like I'm dying. I can't catch my breath through my laughter. Kade's chuckles blending with mine. We sit smiling at each other for more than a little while before Kade breaks the silence.

"Your dad, was he hard on you?"

I hum, wondering how to describe our dynamic. "My dad was used to spending his time with guys. I'm not sure he knew what to do with a little girl."

"He wanted a boy?" Kade asks, his voice hard. I shake my head.

"No. I don't think so. I think he was just happy to be a dad, but when my mom took off, he had to figure out how to raise me on his own while running a business." I tuck my hair behind my ears, remembering how confusing that time was for both of us.

Kade reaches for my hand, and I give it to him without thought. How is it my hand doesn't feel right unless he's holding it?

"When did your mom leave?" he asks quietly.

"I was four, I think. She came back a few times. Dad would take her back each time she came home. She'd stay for a while, then leave again."

His eyes darken. "Was she on drugs?" Of course he'd think that. His mom chose drugs over him every chance she got. Of course he'd think that's why moms leave.

"No, she wasn't as far as I know." I sigh and prop my head in my hand, "I think she just wanted another life." Kade's thumb rubbing over my knuckles is soothing. "They met at a Jiu Jitsu tournament on the west coast. She was majoring in photography and was there to take photos. He always said he fell in love with her the second they met."

"She didn't feel the same?" he guesses.

"I honestly don't know. I remember them being happy for a while. Dad had already started the Dojo in his hometown, so she moved out this way. She got pregnant pretty fast. I was born a little over a year after they met."

I trace my fingers over the white lines on Kade's knuckles. "I think she felt trapped after that. I don't know if she ever wanted to be a mom. She had dreams of being a world-famous photographer, traveling to exotic places for shoots. Life in our town wasn't exotic. It was boring, everyday family stuff."

"Boring everyday family stuff sounds pretty great," Kade says quietly. I nod slowly, looking at those stunning eyes. He's lived such a hard life. Knowing what I know now, I have to agree.

"Yeah, it was."

"Where is she now?"

"She's a world-famous photographer." I snort out a low laugh. "She travels the world. I see her name in magazines sometimes."

Kade's eyes are searching. "How do you feel about that?"

I smile and squeeze his fingers. "I don't really feel much,

to be honest. She sent flowers when Dad died. She sends me a birthday card every year. But I don't really think about her anymore. I'm glad she left, you know? If she couldn't love Dad the way he deserved to be loved, then good riddance. And I guess I'm glad she's doing what she always wanted to do."

"She didn't love you the way you deserve either, Becca."

I have to smile. "True. But honestly, I was so fucking lucky to have my dad. He was there for everything. He read books on puberty and bought period supplies, then explained everything to me." I have to giggle. "You should have seen how red his face was. I don't think he looked me in the eye for a week after that."

Kade doesn't look satisfied with my answer. "Don't you wish she had stayed?"

My smile fades, and I slowly shake my head. "He took such good care of me, Kade. I can't imagine my life any better if she had stayed. She is who she is. Unless she came back a completely different person, someone who desperately wanted to be a wife and mother, there was no way she would have made our world better."

Kade's nodding, looking lost in thought.

I squeeze his hand, drawing his attention back to me.

"My mom is alive and well in the world, living her best life. She made a choice. I understand where you're coming from, though. I'm sure you'd do anything to have your mom back."

Kade slowly drags his hand from mine and leans back in the booth. My hand sits on the table, extended and suddenly cold. I pull it back and tuck it in my lap. I've said something wrong, but I don't know what landmine I've stepped on. I twine my fingers together in my lap, watching the shifting emotions on Kade's face.

His eyes seem to skitter around the restaurant, not settling on anything. His shoulders are tight, the cords in his neck standing out in stark relief. I have the urge to apologize, to smooth things over, but I clench my teeth together to halt the words. I haven't done anything wrong. I know that. But when he goes dark like this, I just want to make it better. Kade exhales a heavy breath, his eyes focused down at the table.

"I…I don't know."

"You don't know…?" I prompt.

Kade's mouth firms before admitting, "I don't know if I'd want her back."

I consciously relax my fingers and lean back in the booth, matching his posture. My silence forces his eyes to meet mine. I make sure my face doesn't betray any feelings. This is not about me, and I know if I show anything on my face, he's going to shut down.

Kade examines my face carefully and must be satisfied with what he sees because his shoulders lower slightly. He clears his throat and reaches to play with the salt and pepper shakers on the table. "My life without my mom was…easier in a lot of ways."

"How?" I ask softly.

"I only had to worry about myself." His smile is sad. "I worried about her so much, Becca. She'd leave for days, then come home so sick. I would go look for her. I sometimes found her. There's an old lot she'd use to…earn the money she needed to buy drugs."

My hands clench into fists at the way he said 'earn.' Jesus, the weight and sadness in that word alone feels like a hundred-pound weight sitting on my chest.

"There were some abandoned houses she'd go to so she could use, too." He's spinning both shakers. They look like miniatures from a child's kitchen set in his large hands. "Sometimes I didn't find her, and I'd have to scrounge for something to eat." Kade laughs softly. "I got stuck in a dumpster once. I climbed the one behind the convenience store, but I didn't realize it was mostly empty until I'd already flipped in. I sat in there all night until someone from the store found me and snatched me out. I ate three boxes of crushed Twinkies that night."

He's examining my face again. I'm really fucking horrified. And so, so sad for him. But I give him a gentle smile and shove the rest of it away. He continues, reassured.

"We never had enough money. She would spend our welfare checks on drugs most of the time, but we sometimes got food from the church or the food bank. I'd steal money from her purse to buy food at the corner store, too. She never noticed."

I slowly place my hand on the table and slide it toward Kade's hands, afraid he might not want the contact. He stills before sliding the shakers to the side of the table. He picks up my hand, cradling it in one of his, using the fingers of the other to trace the blue veins visible on the back.

"And when she was gone?" I ask quietly.

Kade's fingers don't stop their movement. "Micah and I took care of each other. We'd find food together, hustle together. Everything we found, we split. If we couldn't eat that night, Micah was right there with me, hungry, too. We were a team." Kade shrugs. "The home was okay. We got fed three squares a day. But it wasn't until Ransom pulled us all together that I finally felt...safe, I guess."

"You guess?"

Kade snorts, "The things we were doing weren't exactly legal, you know? They weren't safe. Fuck, we all carried knives and other...stuff." Kade's wink makes me laugh despite my horror at all he's lived through. But I sober as he continues, "But the nine of us, we took care of each other. It was the first time I ever felt a part of something. Hell, knowing the guys had my back meant I didn't have to sleep with one eye open. Ransom made it his priority to make sure we were taken care of. He took responsibility for us, even though he was barely older than we were."

Kade's eyes lock on mine. "He still takes care of us. Everything we've built. It's because Ransom wanted better for us all. He dragged us, sometimes literally, into this business. He wanted money because that meant power and control." Kade taps the top of my hand. "We got it."

"The power and control?"

Kade nods. "And the money."

"So he built a business and made sure you all had a place in it." I want to meet this mysterious Ransom.

"We built the business."

I tilt my head in confusion. "Isn't that what I just said?"

Kade's low chuckle dances up my neck. "We all worked in it, yeah, but ownership of Brash Auto…well, the Brash Group is actually split nine ways. We all have an equal share. It's not just his."

I swallow carefully. "So what does the Brash Group do?"

"Owns all the Brash Auto's. Ransom's got us in commercial real estate. He's talking about developing some high-end communities. He even built a fucking high rise for us all."

Jesus.

And I was sleeping in my car a few weeks ago. I thought the distance between our financial situations wouldn't matter, but this isn't just a few blocks.

It's the fucking Grand Canyon.

My voice comes out a little higher than I would have liked. "You own a high-rise?" Kade shrugs casually, like I just asked him if he owns a blue shirt.

"Yeah. Ransom lives in the penthouse at the top. We all spend time there. Then there are two apartments per floor below that for us. Then there are smaller units in the building we sold." My mouth is dry.

"How many floors?" Kade's eyes are sharp, laser-focused on mine.

"Forty," he says shortly.

Well shit. This guy is so far out of my league. It's past funny and moved straight into ridiculous.

"Billionaires build high-rises," I whisper.

Kade's eyes narrow. "Yeah," he says simply.

18

BECCA

I try to pull my hand from his. He tightens his grip but finally lets me pull away. His eyes darken, and the tick is back in his jaw.

My thoughts are swirling but keep coming back to one simple thought.

"This can't go anywhere," I say, my throat tight.

"Explain," Kade demands, his eyes cold.

I shift uncomfortably, collecting my thoughts before answering. "I…maybe I was turning this," I gesture between the two of us, "into more than you ever intended it to be. But I have never felt like this about anyone before, Kade. You have this way of looking at me that makes me feel like the most stunning woman in the world. And when you're in the room, everything else disappears for me." His brows relax. I tuck my hair behind my ears and clear my throat. "I think I built a bit of a dream about what a life together could look like. But I'm realizing that maybe it's a bit of a pipe dream."

"A pipe dream?" Kade asks gruffly. His eyes aren't arctic anymore, but I miss the warmth he was looking at me with before. I blink back the moisture in my eyes, already grieving my dream.

"I had a small life, Kade. I traveled some, saw the world some, but I always came back home. I liked being at the Dojo. Having dinner with Dad, doing yard work on the weekends. It was simple and routine. And I loved it. If Dad hadn't died, I would have stayed forever." I smile, thinking of it. "I would have eventually gotten married and bought a house a block or two away. Maybe have a few kids. Raised some badasses."

Kade's finger is tapping on the table in a steady rhythm. "And you don't see that with me," he says flatly.

"You're a billionaire. I can't even picture how much money that is. Offering to fix my car…well fuck, you probably make three thousand dollars in interest in a day."

His voice is impersonal, "More like five minutes."

Holy crap.

"You are so out of my league. That restaurant we were at tonight. That's where people like you eat. You drive expensive cars, go on exotic vacations. You have people mow your lawns and clean your houses. That life…it's not for me."

Kade nods slowly, grinding his teeth. "You don't want to live the life of an entitled, lazy, rich asshole."

No. I really don't. Flashes of vapid celebrities and reality shows flash through my mind.

"Ah…I wouldn't have put it just like that, but…yes," I admit, hurrying to add, "I don't think you're lazy or entitled. But your life is on a trajectory that…well, just looking at the dresses the women in that restaurant stuffed themselves into makes my skin itch. I like leggings. And T-shirts. And hot dogs."

Hot dogs? Really Becca? I want to slap myself in the face.

Kade's expression shuts down, and he nods again. "Right. So you don't want to wear expensive clothes and go to fancy restaurants. You don't want to live in a high-rise or go on expensive vacations. So because of those things, you're what…dumping me? You realize every other woman I've met wants those things, right? They would do anything for them."

I sound stupid. It is stupid. And they're just excuses. And I'm hurting him. I risk a glance at Kade's angry face before dropping my eyes to the table and telling him the truth of it.

"I would embarrass you, Kade." I hate that it's true. I hate saying it. "You need a poised, sophisticated woman. Someone who can walk into any room with you and have all those rich, snooty people eating out of her hand. Someone who could be an asset to you." I sigh and raise my eyes to his blazing ones. "I crapped my pants when I was eight. I always say the wrong thing. I will never have the body of a supermodel. And I don't want to live in a world where I'll always feel less than."

I'm tempted to break under Kade's relentless stare, but I've never backed down from the truth. I won't now. We sit, staring for an eternity before he finally speaks.

"Who the fuck do you think I am?" His words are clipped, hard. He doesn't wait for me to answer. "I ate out of a fucking dumpster, Becca. My mother was a junkie. I can't even remember every crime I've committed, there's been so many. I've been shot at and stabbed. And now, when I walk into an expensive restaurant, everybody knows who I am."

He leans forward, flattening his hands on the table.

"And I. Don't. Give. A. Fuck."

Kade's eyes are blazing, but not with anger. "You think you'll feel less than? That's your fucking baggage. I know. I've been there. It was a long road to our first million. Then it was a fucking runaway freight train. We were rich before we knew it. So yeah, we did all the rich stuff. We bought planes. Went to ten thousand dollar plate dinners, went to fucking Ibiza. And you know what, Becca?"

I shake my head, his intensity stealing my breath.

"I fucking hated it. I hated how shallow most people were. I hated fucking caviar. I hated the stupid fucking galas.

We all did." Kade leans slowly back in the booth, continuing in a quieter voice. "We've walked through fire to get where we are. I have nothing in common with most of those people. Their worst day is a walk in the fucking park compared to what we've lived through. So you don't want to feel less than? That's your fucked up shit to handle. Because you're already way fucking better than they are. Way stronger."

I swallow thickly, his words rattling in my chest. I can't tear my eyes from his.

"You were dreaming about us, Becca?" he asks gently, his anger fizzled out.

I nod dumbly, my mind spinning. Kade smiles slowly.

"What did you dream?"

I feel the flush rising in my chest. I feel naked. Exposed. Admitting everything I had dreamed about the last few weeks feels like too much. I shrug helplessly.

Kade's smile softens. "I've never been with anyone like you, Becca. You're the first woman I've been with that I could see...more...with. I'm pretty fucking gone for you, in case you haven't noticed." He leans forward, crossing his arms and resting them on the table. "You got me thinking things, Bec. You got me wanting to make plans. So tell me, beautiful Becca, what were you dreaming?"

I blow out a breath, then look him straight in the eye.

"They're not big dreams, Kade. I was thinking about road trips. And sleeping in on Sunday mornings. And making dinner together." I smile. "And arguing about what movie we'll go see. And maybe someday having a house and kids. It's trick-or-treating and family dinners and Christmas morning." Kade's eyes are fixed on mine. He doesn't look scared off. If anything, he looks...intrigued.

"I've never had most of those things, Becca. But how the fuck does me being rich mean I can't have them now?"

"Ah...well, your life seems so much bigger than all of

that." That sounds pretty thin, even to my ears. Kade shakes his head and waves his hand around the room.

"This is my life, Becca. I go to work and I go home. I may put a fucking suit on, but at the end of the day, I'm in jeans and a T-shirt. And I'm with you. What is it that's so big about my life?"

That sounds pretty great. What is the problem with that?

"Well, what about when you have to go to some business dinner and need your girlfriend to go with you?"

Kade tilts his head at me in confusion. "What part of 'I fucking hated it' are you not getting? If there's something I want you to come to, I'll fucking ask you. You don't want to go, you say no."

That seems way too easy.

"Kade, I've seen what it does to a relationship when two people want different things. It destroyed my mom and dad's marriage. I don't want that for myself."

"I don't have any fucking expectations, Becca," Kade growls.

"Seriously? How does that work, then? You have to go to some fancy gala and if I don't want to go, you what? Take a date instead?"

Kade snorts and looks at me, his frustration with me written all over his face. "Why is this concept so fucking hard for you to understand? And why are you still talking about fucking galas? I don't want to go to some gala. I'm a fucking billionaire, and that means I don't have to go anywhere I don't want to." He winces and clarifies, "Well, unless my brothers need me. Then I go. And if they're asking me to go to some fucking ritzy party then it's for a damned good reason, so I'll go."

"So you have no expectations of me at all?"

"No," Kade says firmly.

Huh. While I'm relieved, I'm also a little worried. How does a relationship work when one person doesn't have any expectations of the other? It's completely unrealistic. I study Kade. He looks more than finished with this conversation. A smart woman would probably just let this go, smooth it over, and carry on as if everything was fine. I don't do that.

"You should have expectations of me, Kade," I tell him firmly. I ignore his growl. "Seriously. What do you need in a relationship?" Jesus, the confusion on his face is heartbreaking. Does he not realize that he deserves things too? That relationships are supposed to be a two way street? "How do you want to be treated, Kade? What does your partner need to do for you to make you feel loved? What do you want life to look like a year from now? Hell, five years from now."

My heart breaks a little bit looking at him. He looks lost. Like he's never considered what he might need in a relationship.

"Things are okay, aren't they, Becca?" he asks, his voice hesitant.

I sigh, "I know this is new, Kade. We still don't know that much about each other. But in the last month, I've caught feelings. And I really want to see where this could go. Honestly, I think it's pretty great so far. I think it could keep getting better. But," I tear my eyes away and focus on a scratch on the table, "if that's not what you want, if you don't see the possibility of a future, then I'd really appreciate you telling me."

"And if I don't see a future, Bec?" My heart drops. I knew this was a possibility, that I was building us up to be bigger than we truly are.

"Then we stop seeing each other, Kade. If you don't see this going anywhere. If your feelings aren't growing like mine are. Then I need you to be honest about that before I fall all the way in love with you."

Kade's arms drop from the table, and he leans back in the booth, scratching the stubble on his chin.

"Fuck...you're not one to just...coast, are you?" His brows are drawn.

I shrug, steeling myself. "I don't want to live my life with regrets, Kade. What we have together? It's so good. I want more of it. I want more of you. And I know I flipped out a little. I'm sorry, the whole mega-rich thing threw me a bit. It's an obstacle, but clearly, one we can get over. But if your feelings for me aren't growing the way mine are for you ... well, I don't think I can get over that. I want the big love, Kade. I want to find the person who will hold my hand in fifty years, telling me how beautiful I am, dentures and all." His mouth quirks before turning down again. Kade sighs and drops his hands on the table. He looks torn.

"Becca, I've never seen that. I'm not sure I believe it exists." I swallow past the emotion in my throat, sad for him all over again. Sad for me. "But I've also never been in a relationship like this before. With someone like you. You're pretty fucking strong, Becca. And you have your shit together in a way no one I've ever dated has. The picture you're painting sounds pretty great. And I don't want to lose you, but..."

The backs of my eyelids are burning. "But you're not there yet."

He shakes his head slowly. "No. That doesn't mean I won't get there. My fucking feelings for you are big. But I..." His chest deflates, and he pushes his hands through his hair in agitation. "Can you give me a bit of fucking time? I just need to catch up a bit." He reaches across the table, his hand searching for mine. I let him take it. I want to feel his warmth wrapping around mine. "I don't want you going anywhere. I want more of this. Can that be enough for now? Please, Becca."

Can it be enough for now? If it's not, then that means walking away. The idea of walking away from him, from the electricity between us, is agonizing. But I lied a little. I'm not falling in love with him. I've already fallen. I'm fucked already. If I walk away, I'll break my own heart. And if I don't walk? Well, maybe, if I'm patient, I could get my forever. I think he's worth it.

We're worth it.

I tighten my fingers around Kade's and smile. "Yes, it's enough."

19

BECCA

When I first started at the new Dojo, I was worried it wouldn't live up to my expectations. Dad had set a pretty high bar, but Devin and Jeff are dedicated to their students and, by the end of the first week, gave into my urging to create a women's self-defense class.

I didn't have to try that hard to convince them, and I was grateful for the chance to bring something from home here. My self-defense classes back home were always full. Without fail, at the end of every twelve-week session, a woman would come up and tell me I'd changed her life. Because of the things she'd learned in my class, she felt safer. Stronger. More capable.

The women who turn up to my classes usually fall into one of two groups. First, women who want to be prepared. They're usually excited, laughing, and hooting their way through the class. They walk through the space with confidence, unaware of their vulnerability, mostly untouched by violence.

Second, women who have been or are being hurt. They carry themselves with a fragility that the first group can't understand. I can almost always spot them in the first class.

These women stick to the back of the room. They avoid eye contact and cling to their long sleeve shirts. Their eyes darting left and right as they move through the space. They approach the drills in class the way a marine approaches basic training. Like it's their job. I always find myself paying a little more attention to those women.

I knew the moment Holly walked into my first class that she fell into group two. Despite her generous curves, she was small. And so soft-spoken, I would have to strain to hear her. I formed a habit of walking her out after class, chatting with her at the bus stop. She looked like she needed a friend. And honestly, so did I.

I'd tried to reconnect with some of my old friends, but the conversations were stilted. We were different people now. Dad's death damaged those relationships in a way that can never be fully fixed. I was drawn to Holly because, despite the clear hurt she'd experienced, her kindness and warmth shone through. I felt warm just being near her. It took me a few classes, but I cracked Holly's shell a bit and convinced her to hang out with me. I wanted to know more about her.

I really, really wanted to know if she was safe.

And when I told Kade that, he didn't try to convince me to change my mind and spend the night with him. Instead, he left me with a kiss and a "stay safe." That man, I swear it was getting harder and harder to remember my plan to wait. Kade seems to soak up every minute with me, wanting all the time I can give him. I want all his time too. All his hot, hungry looks. All his sneaky touches in the office and the long, slow, drugging kisses. But he's still holding back, and I know the wall between us isn't mine to scale.

I let Holly into my apartment, sliding the pizza and beer onto the counter.

"Grab a couple of glasses…cupboard to the left of the stove," I invite her as I kick my shoes into the corner.

Holly stretches up on her toes to reach the glasses on the second shelf, and I'm reminded again of how tiny she really is.

"How tall are you, Hol?" I ask. She grimaces.

"Five-foot, three-quarter inches." She sighs as she continues, "Since the seventh grade."

I can't help but giggle at the disgust on her face. She scrunches up her nose, putting her hands on her hips.

"I'm sorry. I'm not laughing at you. You just sound so pissed," I say as I cover my mouth. She frowns at me, but I see her lip curling up.

"Try riding a packed bus in the middle of summer." She raises her arm to demonstrate, "Everyone standing and holding the straps…yep, I'm armpit level." She shudders, and I let my body fold forward, the laughter rolling out uncontrollably.

"Jesus, Holly, that's awful." I shudder, too, imagining the stench of a city bus at rush hour in 100-degree heat. I wipe my eyes as I pull plates down for us, serving us each two pieces. Holly pours the beers, and we slump onto the sofa, giggling and chatting our way through the meal.

"God!" I exclaim. "I'm so glad you're here. I've missed just hanging out with friends."

Holly smiles. "You miss your friends back home?"

I almost say yes, but stop. "Not really," I admit. Holly tilts her head in confusion. "I had some great friends," I explain, "but, well, we've drifted apart over the last year."

"Why?" she asks softly.

I set my last slice back on my plate. "My dad got really sick and died," She doesn't say anything. Just puts her small hand on my knee. Her eyes are filled with sympathy.

I feel my tears rise as I soak in her compassion. I need this. I need to talk about Dad. Kade and I have talked about everything this week, but I've avoided this conversation with him, not wanting to be that vulnerable when things feel so unsteady. I don't want him to go back to thinking he needs to fix me, and I'm pretty sure crying in front of him would be bad at this stage of our relationship.

"Tell me," she orders softly.

So I do.

I tell her about how tired he was. How the doctor ordered a million tests immediately. I told her about the awful wait, trying to stay hopeful, but knowing the urgency of the tests meant things weren't good. I tell her about the Stage Four diagnosis.

"It was so awful, Holly," I say, scrubbing my wet cheeks. "It was too far gone. The cancer was everywhere. They tried some chemo and radiation. They said it might buy him time, but it made him so sick."

I sob, remembering him curled on the bathroom floor, a shadow of the strong Daddy I always knew him to be. "He was so tired, Holly. So I brought him home, and I took care of him until the end."

Her hand is rubbing my knee, and I focus on that soothing touch as I get my breathing under control. "And then…" she prompts softly.

I sigh and rest my head on the back of the couch. "I tried to make things work for a while. The Dojo was limping along, some of the older students taking over a few classes. But I just couldn't be there anymore. The whole town was filled with memories. I wanted to drive down the street and not be hit by them everywhere I looked. And my friends, well, they couldn't handle my sadness. They didn't know what to say, how to act, and they just," I wiggled my fingers, "drifted away."

I rub my cheek remembering the way my friends would wince and look guilty when I saw them in town. "So I sold the house. And closed down the Dojo. I had just enough to pay off his medical bills and my overdue credit card accounts."

There was so much debt. The collection calls were giving me a fucking ulcer. In hindsight, it would have been smarter to keep at least one credit card. But nope, I had to go and shut them all. "Then I packed up everything I could fit in my piece of shit car and left." I shrug. "And here I am."

We sit for a while, comfortable in the silence, until Holly breaks it.

"You're so brave."

I snort, feeling like a coward. "I ran Holly. That's not brave."

Her hand grips my arm, and I shift to look at her grave face. "That's not what you tell us in class, Becca." I flush. That's true. Avoiding a fight, getting away, is the smartest thing you can do to stay safe. "Sometimes running is the bravest thing you can do," she finishes softly. I see she means it. And that she knows exactly what she's talking about.

"You ran too," I breathe. It's not a question, and I don't mean she ran from memories. She knows that.

"Yeah, I did. It took me longer than I wish it had, but I got away." I lean toward her, gripping her hand.

"Are you safe now?" She shrugs, the acceptance on her face killing me.

"I'm safe for now. That's as good as it's going to get for me." I want to tell her she's wrong. That she can be completely safe. But I can't argue with the certainty on her face. I reach out and take her hand.

"Make me a promise, Holly." She studies me, and I sit silent and patient under her gaze. She nods finally, and I let out the breath I didn't realize I was holding. "Promise me that if you're no longer safe, you'll let me know." She breaks eye contact and stares over my shoulder for what feels like years before finally nodding. I squeeze her hand. "Thank you."

I grab us another beer, and over the next hour, we slide

into a deeper friendship. Maybe deeper than I ever have before. There's something about sharing the darkest part of yourself with someone, knowing that they've stood in the darkness too, that lets you skip past the superficial and dive into a genuine friendship.

"You kiddin' me!" I exclaim. "You should report his dis… disgu…gross ass, Holly. He sounds like a piece of sheeeet." I'm past tipsy, heading all the way to karaoke drunk, so it comes out louder than I realize.

Holly blows a raspberry in agreement and ends up spitting down her shirt, making me giggle, snort, and spill my beer, which then makes her giggle-snort.

Soon we're in a giggle-snort spiral, leaning against each other, shaking, crying, laughing. I haven't laughed this much in forever. I sigh, then sit up quickly, tipping Holly onto the floor, making her snort some more. I reach down and pull her back on the couch, patting her down to put everything back into place. She slaps my hands away from her boobs, and I laugh again

"Sorry!" My head feels fuzzy, but I had a great… "You should quit your shitty job and work here!" I exclaim. It's perfect! I'm the most genius of all the genius people in the world. Holly slid down the couch, her chin resting on her chest.

"Huh?" She asks with one eye open.

"It's such a good idea, Holly. I'm so smart," I tell her earnestly. "I can't find any smart people to take my job here. You'd do so good! You're smart. And pretty. And smart." I nod. I keep nodding till the bobbing of my head makes me feel like I'm going to puke. I grab it to hold it steady.

"What do I have to do for the work?" Holly slurs.

I put my finger in her face. "You have to do the papers, then order the thingys and then take the money. K?"

Holly nods, "K."

Good. That's settled. I tip over till my head rests on hers, and we sink into sleep.

IT TAKES A LITTLE MORE CONVINCING IN THE MORNING, BUT BY the time lunch rolls around the next day, I have Holly convinced to come work at Brash. She's not going to give her piece of shit boss any notice—the creeper doesn't deserve any. And in the clear light of day, my idea is still genius. Holly will be perfect for the job.

20

BECCA

I wave frantically at Holly through the office window. She's going to be so great here. Her smile is nervous as she pulls open the door. I can't contain a little squeal.

"I'm so glad you're here. This is going to be so great!" It really is. I can feel it. Holly needs this place. I've warned all the guys to be on their best behavior. She's skittish, and I don't want them giving her any reason to leave.

Besides, I know she'll be way better off working here. The fuckery going on at her old job was not okay. I don't know everything she's been through, but no way should she be treated like that. No woman should ever feel unsafe at her job, or anywhere else, for that matter.

Personally, I'm thrilled she's here because that means I'm one step closer to quitting. I'm ready to be at the Dojo full time. Working in both places has made it hard to spend much time with Kade, and it's getting harder and harder to hold back with him. There's been some serious making out, but I've kept my pants on to make sure I didn't give in to temptation. Course, I made sure to wear stretchy pants so Kade could get his hands inside.

But rolling around on my couch is not cutting it anymore.

I feel like a teenager again, sneaking moments with my boyfriend. Saying goodnight to him and watching him walk away is killing me. I want him in my bed. Under me, over me, in me. Holly taking over here means I'm that much closer to sitting on his face.

"I'm a little nervous," Holly admits.

I smile and wrap my arm around her shoulders, drawing her away from the door. "You're going to do so well, Holly. I promise you have nothing to worry about," I reassure her. "C'mon, let's get your stuff put away, and I'll introduce you around."

Most of the guys have been working for an hour. I didn't want Holly to come in during the morning rush on her first day and feel overwhelmed. I show her the drawer she can keep her purse in, then check the parking area to make sure no customers are in sight before leading her into the garage bays.

I introduce her to the mechanics, feeling proud as I watch her smile at them, chatting, looking so fresh and adorable. She's so tiny. She's wearing a cute yellow dress that falls to her shins and three-inch nude heels to make her a little taller. She looks like a daisy.

As she wraps up with the last guy, I smile and check-in. "How are you doing so far?"

The nerves in her smile have dissipated. "Good. They're all so nice!" Her joy in being here is shining through.

"I'm so glad, Hol. Let's go find Micah." As I head toward Micah's work area in the far bay, I prep her. "Micah doesn't talk much, Holly. It's nothing personal. It's just hard for him to talk sometimes."

I glance back and see the concern on her face. "Is he injured?"

I'm not sure how to answer that without breaking Micah's trust. In the end, I settle for, "He was. He's okay now, but it left some damage. Don't worry, though. We've got a system worked out to communicate, and I'm sure you'll pick it up easily." Holly is one of the kindest people I've met. I know she'll do whatever she needs to work with Micah.

I spot him on the far side of his current project car. He's crouched down, doing something in the wheel wells, only the top of his head visible. I wave at Holly to follow and go around the car.

"Hey, dude."

He smiles, still working in the well, and mutters, "Hey," back.

"I want you to meet Holly. She's going to be taking over for me." His smile falls, and he takes a deep breath before looking up. He glances at me, resignation in his eyes, before letting them drift past me to Holly. His eyes widen, and his body freezes.

"Hello," Holly says softly, smiling gently at Micah. I step to the side, turning to face both of them.

"Holly, this is Micah. Restoration expert. Man of many talents, man of few words." I do some jazz hands, and Holly laughs at me a bit. "Micah, this is Holly. She's pretty much the nicest person I've ever met," I tell him honestly.

Micah's eyes are still locked on Holly. "Woah…hi," he breathes.

Oh. My. God.

He's blushing.

I've never been able to make him blush, not even with the dirtiest jokes in my repetoire. Holly flushes and looks away before darting her eyes back to Micah. A little smile is still teasing the corner of her mouth. She bites the corner of her lip and takes a small step forward, extending her hand. Interesting. She didn't offer to shake anyone else's hand.

Micah gulps and reaches for her hand as he stands to his full six-five. Holly gasps and stumbles back a step. Her heel catches on the grate in the floor, and she starts to fall. Before I can move, Micah's big arms wrap around her and pull her into his chest. She looks like a child, held against him. Well, a very curvy, boobalicious, child anyway. I'm just about to tease them a bit when I glimpse Holly's face. Her eyes are glazed, and her face is bone white. Her hands, down at her sides, are clenched into tight fists.

I've seen this before.

"Holly," I say calmly, "you're okay. I'm right here, and Micah would never hurt you." I reach out and put my palm firmly on her shoulder. "Put her down," I say quietly to Micah.

He looks like he's in pain, his eyes searching Holly's frozen features. He slowly unwraps his arms from her, making sure her feet are steady on the ground. Even in her heels, the top of her head only comes up to his armpit. I slowly slide my arm over her shoulders.

"Deep breath Holly. In with me. Come on now." I take a deep breath in, encouraging her until she shudders and takes a deep breath. "Good. Let it out really slowly now."

We breathe together for a few minutes. My focus is on Holly, but I'm conscious of Micah breathing with us. His thick chest moving in time with ours. I want to reassure him he did nothing wrong, but I won't take my attention from Holly. "Give me three things, Holly," I push her, wanting her to check in with her surroundings. "Just three."

She takes another deep breath before muttering, "Your hand on my back...laughter...oranges." I smile, knowing she's smelling the guys' soap.

"Good. Do you need another minute?"

She nods, her eyes now focused on the floor. I shift my body, sheltering her from Micah's gaze. He growls, and I shoot him a 'shut the fuck up' scowl over my shoulder. Holly's quiet voice brings my head to hers.

"I'm so embarrassed." I can hear the tears in her voice, and I feel so fucking angry at the piece of shit that hurt her.

"You have absolutely nothing to be sorry for, you hear

me?" My voice is firm. Sure. "Look at me, Holly." I wait until her eyes meet mine. "You are not to blame for this reaction. It's instinctive. You were triggered. The only thing you have to do is breathe and find your balance. However you need to do that is fine."

I can sense Micah's anxiety behind me, but I don't want to take my attention off Holly. I'm so angry that she has to deal with shit like this, but I know she's on a long road to healing, and triggers are gonna happen for her no matter what.

"Holly, it's really okay," I tell her. She nods, sniffs, then smooths down her dress. Her hands come up and quickly wipe away the moisture on her face. She takes a deep breath, then gently nudges me away.

"Micah, I apologize," she says, looking up at him. "My reaction was uncalled for." Micah's features are tight. He puts his fist on his chest and makes a circular motion. "You have nothing to be sorry for, Micah. You didn't do anything wrong. Thank you for making sure I didn't fall."

Wait. What?

"What do you mean he doesn't have to apologize? He apologized?" Micah's eyes are as wide as mine. Holly smiles at me and makes the same circular motion over her chest.

"That's 'sorry' in ASL."

Well, fuck me sideways.

"Holly, how did you know Micah uses ASL? I didn't tell you! I'm still trying to learn, and I didn't want to overwhelm you."

She shrugs. "One of my best friends as a child was deaf. I started learning in elementary school." She looks at Micah again, her color still high. "I haven't used it in a while, but I'll make sure I brush up, okay?"

Micah nods, eyes still wide. "Okay…Holly." They just stand there staring at each other, and I'm left feeling like a third wheel.

I clap my hands. "Okay…Holly, let's head back to the

office so we can start training." Micah tears his eyes from Holly's, nods, and crouches back to the wheel well.

I lead Holly back to the office. She heads to the drawer with her purse and pulls out a compact to check her face. She's avoiding my eyes. I watch her fuss for a while before confronting her. "What happened in there?"

"Can you be more specific?" she asks, still not looking at me.

I chuckle. "Holly and Micah sitting in a tree, K-I-S..." I'm belly laughing as Holly's small hands press against my mouth.

"Shut your big fat mouth, Becca!"

I pry her hands off my mouth, still laughing. "Okay. Okay." My giggles fade along with my smile. "But seriously, Holly, what triggered you?"

She crosses her arms over her chest, rubbing her biceps. "I didn't realize he was so big...I got startled."

"And that's it?" I think there's more to it.

She sighs, "Well when he...wrapped me up, I panicked." I nod, giving her the space to say more if she wants. "My... husband...he used to pick me up and..." Her voice trails off.

I have to struggle to keep my anger for her out of my voice. "Got it Hol. Thank you for sharing with me."

She nods and drops her arms. "Okay, what do I need to learn first?"

21

KADE

"**K**ade! Hold Up." Declan's voice stops me on the way to my office.

I swing around and head into his cave. When Ransom bought this building and turned it into the Brash Auto compound, he insisted that we all have an office here. He put a fancy desk and chairs in every office, but that's where the similarities between them end. Ransom and I have kept our offices pretty simple and client-ready. Micah's has never been used.

Declan's though?

It looks like the fucking bat cave. He keeps his blinds down and has a six monitor setup going. I don't know what the hell he needs with six monitors, but when he explained to me what they were all for, I zoned the fuck out. When I walk in, he's kicked back in his chair, feet on the desk, keyboard on his lap. He's wearing his usual jeans, so old they're almost white, a grey T-shirt, and a plain black hoodie. He's been wearing a variation of that outfit for the last twenty years.

"What's up, fucker?"

Dec gives me the finger. "C'mere, douchenozzle."

That's a new one.

When you grow up with eight other guys, swearing becomes an integral part of your vocabulary. Add in working in a garage? Well, we're fucking hopeless. But douchenozzle?

I chuckle as I round the desk, sitting on the filing cabinet next to him, punching him on the shoulder as I pass. "You're getting bigger, man. You been working out with Colt? No way you're getting muscles like that sitting on your ass."

Declan snorts. "Me and Jonas have a bet."

I laugh, wondering what stupidity they're up to now. Their last bet resulted in a fucking ridiculous tattoo on Declan's ass. "What is it this time? It's not like Jonas to be in the gym."

"Nope. But he read some fucking study…studies…on the health benefits of body weight exercises for men, and he's decided that we need to get pumped. Dickhead wouldn't let up. He kept leaving copies of the studies highlighted on my desk."

"And what? You read them and agreed?"

"Fuck no! I ignored them."

Oh, this is going to be good.

"And…?"

Declan growls and mutters, "Fucker knocked on my door at six am. He wouldn't let the fuck up until I went to the gym with him."

I don't even try to hide my grin. "How long did he knock?"

Dec huffs in frustration before admitting, "Twenty minutes. I thought for sure he'd give up after ten but nope."

I lean forward, letting the laughter roll through me. "Of course he did. When have you ever known Jonas to give up."

Dec scowls at me, but I see a hint of a smile peeking through. "So, what's the bet?"

"First one to fifteen thousand muscle ups."

I whistle thinking of the fucking upper body strength that

takes. "And the loser?" Declan laughs like a cartoon villain. "Loser has to get a mohawk and dye it bright red."

I snort and pat him on the shoulder. "Don't worry, man. You can pull off a mohawk. The red? Not so sure."

He drops his feet from the desk and scowls at me. "Fuckhead! Why the hell do you think I'm going to lose?"

"Seriously, man?" I ask him. How can he think he'll win?

"Yes, seriously," he says, flexing his muscles, "I'm already in way better shape than Jonas is. Fucker barely worked out before this."

"Remember the bet he made with Maverick?" How can he forget the fucking consequences of losing a bet with Jonas?

His face whitens, and he sucks in a breath. "Christ. I'm fucked," Declan mutters, running his fingers through his shaggy hair.

"Yeah. You are." I give him a minute to wallow in his inevitable defeat before I check my watch and kick the bottom of his chair. "Why am I here?"

"Why are any of us here, man? That is the question. You know I watched this docume- Hey shithead, that's my favorite bobblehead. Don't you fucking dare throw that!"

I hold the Yoda bobble head high, just out of his reach. "Get to the fucking point, Declan. I've got somewhere to be."

A deep chuckle turns our heads to the door. Ransom's leaning on the door jam, his colossal frame filling the doorway.

"Ran," we both mutter in greeting. He's only thirty-eight, but he's somehow always felt like a parent to me. To all of us. I lower the bobblehead and clear my throat. "Dec, I really do need to get going."

Declan nods and sits up straighter. "So listen, I got some info on that scammer chick you asked me to run."

I lean forward, eager to know more. "Tell me." I'm aware of Ransom dropping into the chair across from the desk, but my attention stays on Declan.

"So the woman is a serial con artist. Your girl is not the first person she's pulled this roommate scam on."

I tense at 'your girl,' and I see Ransom straighten in his chair. Fuck, now I feel like I'm in trouble.

"Anyway. I managed to track her down. She runs scams with a loser guy. I think he's her boyfriend."

My hands clench at the news. Finally. He found her. Becca deserves to get her money back. I hate that this bitch took advantage of her, and I want payback.

"Give me her info. I'll run her down." With pleasure.

"No can do, man. Colt was with me when I was running it. He's dealing with it." I want to argue, but I know Colt is more than capable of getting the fucking money back. I just don't want him to be the one fixing this for Becca. That's supposed to be my job.

"Kade," Ransom's deep voice interrupts. I reluctantly shift my eyes to his. "Your girl?"

I clench my fists before slowly loosening them. "Yeah. My girl."

Ransom hums. "First I'm hearing of it." He says evenly, but I hear the question in his voice.

I exhale and rub the back of my neck. "Becca is the woman who took over the office at Knight Street."

Ransom's eyebrows raise. "And you're what…dating?"

"Yeah, man, we're dating." I can feel explanations bubbling up, but I remind myself I'm a grown fucking man and don't owe him anything. It doesn't help.

"And you left her in charge of the office?" I nod. Ransom hums again. "And how did you meet her?" I twist my head, cracking my neck. I respect him too much to lie, but fuck, I want to.

"Her car broke down. She was sleeping in it in front of the garage."

"I see." Ransom's voice is deeper, quieter. "And did the car get fixed?"

I sigh. "Yeah, Ran, I fixed it," I admit. I'd had it done by the weekend. Working on it after hours. I still haven't told Becca.

"How much in parts?" he asks carefully.

"Three grand."

Another nod.

Another hum.

I know exactly what he's thinking, and it's pissing me the fuck off.

"And did she pay you for it?"

Some of my anger seeps into my voice. "No, man. She doesn't know it's fixed."

"I see. So she has no car. Declan mentioned the roommate scam. So I'm guessing she had nowhere to live?"

I nod, body tense.

"So she's staying in the apartment, right?" I nod again. Declan slides his chair back, leaving a clear line of sight between Ransom and me. Ransom's sigh peels a layer off my skin.

"It's not like that, Ran," I defend, unable to help myself. "She's paying rent."

Ransom rubs his face with his hand. His eyes look tired. "Kade, your heart is too good, man. You can't keep letting these women take advantage of you. You gave her access to the shop? To the money? For fuck's sake, man. Get your head out of your ass."

I feel my face heat, remembering all the times he's had to pull me out of a relationship mess. It's happened too often. And it makes me feel like a fucking idiot.

"It's not like that, man. She's different."

"You always say that, Kade," he says, sounding tired.

I do always say that.

When I paid for Victoria's rehab the first time, I said the same thing.

Also said it when I was dating Carly before she tried to

steal an entire wheeled rack full of tools from the garage. I still don't know what the fuck she was thinking, but she managed to catch one of the wheels on a grate in the parking lot and spill the whole fucking thing. Micah watched it happen, and the boys about pissed themselves, watching the security footage on a loop after. They still haven't let me live it down.

I play it off like it's no big deal, but it's fucking embarrassing. I feel stupid every time I think about it. Carly didn't start out that way. She was sweet. She had this funny little giggle that drew me in. She talked softly, and she really fucking seemed to care about me. Hell, at the time, I thought we were perfect. But in the end, I wasn't enough, and she went off the fucking rails.

I exhale heavily. "I know. But she really is different, Ran." She has to be. I need her to be so fucking badly. I need her to be the one to finally choose me. "She's really fucking smart. The shop is running better than it ever has. You can ask Jonas. And she's clean. You ran her background Dec. Tell him."

Declan nods his head. "It's true, man. I ran her right away. She's got no record. She's completely clean. Her finances were fucked, but they're clean now too. She's down on her luck, but it's new."

Ransom shifts his eyes between us. "What happened?"

I let Declan answer. "Her dad died. She had to sell everything to pay off his medical bills. She was left with nothing."

Ransom's features relax a fraction.

"She's a good woman," I tell him quietly. "She's found another job, but she's training a friend of hers to take over for her at the garage."

Declan whistles, his eyes going stormy. "Holly. Her fucking background check made me want to commit murder."

Ransom and I both straighten.

"What?" I ask harshly.

"There was something off with her. The name and ID she gave on her employment application are fakes. Good fakes." He smiles. "But not good enough to fool me. I pulled a few threads and unraveled it pretty quick. I found nine-one-one calls and police reports that never got filed. And medical records." He swallows, his smile fading. "I stopped after that. She's running, but she's not a harm to us. But someone hurt her…my guess is her fucking husband."

"Shit," I mutter. "Becca met her at her self-defense class." I wince. "She's really fucking tiny, Ransom. Barely five feet. Any man hitting her is going to do serious damage."

Ransom's jaw is clenched. "Keep an eye on it, Dec," he bites off.

Declan nods. "Will do."

Ransom sighs and stands, moving to leave. He stops in the doorway, turning back to speak. "Kade, can I talk with you outside, please?"

I nod my thanks to Declan, then, with heavy feet, follow Ransom into the empty hallway.

"I feel like I'm getting called to the fucking principal's office, Ran."

Ransom sighs, the corner of his eyes narrowing. "I'm not your fucking principal. And you're not in trouble. You're a grown man, for fuck's sake," he says, echoing my thoughts from earlier.

"I know I am, but I fucking hate it when you look at me like that."

"How am I looking at you?" he challenges.

"Like you're disappointed in me," I say, rubbing my hand on the back of my head. "Like I'm a fuckup."

Ransom shifts, his eyes staring down the hallway sightlessly. He exhales, a big tired sounding breath. "This was never part of the fucking plan, Kade."

"What plan is that, exactly?"

He shrugs one shoulder, then leans against the wall.

"This," he says, waving to the office around us, "you, the rest of the guys, all of you treating me like I'm your fucking father. That wasn't part of the plan."

He looks tired. More tired than I've ever seen him. His shoulders are rolled forward like he's carrying a thousand pounds on his back. He's always carried his burdens without bowing. A little thread of fear unwinds in my gut. What's happening with him? Why is he so weighed down?

"There's a lot to unpack there, man. But…which plan are we talking about?" Ransom's eyes shift to me, pinning me in place.

"When I chose you guys in that fucking place. When I pulled us all together, it wasn't so I could be your dad. That was never part of the plan. I wanted…" He trails off.

"What did you want?" I ask quietly. He looks at me, and I can almost see a reel of our history playing back in his eyes.

"I wanted a family. A strong one."

I swallow thickly and nod. "You built one man. The fucking strongest."

And he did. There's no fucking way we'd all be where we are today without him. He's got to know that. "You know that we're all here with big fat mansion-sized bank accounts because of you, right?"

His dark eyebrows slash down. "We all fucking built this, Kade."

I shake my head at him. "No, man. I get that you believe that, but we all know differently. We're here because you had a vision. You saw a better life for us all. One bigger than we ever dreamed." I hold up my hand to stop the denials I see sitting on his tongue. "We look up to you because we know we're here because of you. And because you love us, you jackass. We don't want to let you down. And all I ever do is let you down. It's a big fucking pill to swallow." He clenches his jaw, then pushes off the wall, grabbing the back of my neck in his hand, bringing our foreheads together.

"You've never let me down, brother. Not once. So get that fucking thought out of your head."

"The office, the women—" I say past the lump in my throat.

"No." His voice is firm. Unyielding. "Your fucking heart is just too big, Kade. I need you to take better care of it. I don't want to pick up any more of your broken pieces."

"There's not many left," I admit quietly.

Ransom growls, "There's enough, man. You're enough."

I have to close my stinging eyes. Ransom may not get why we look up to him, but it's this. This care he always shows. This driving need he has for us to be okay. No wonder he's fucking exhausted. We're a whole hell of a lot for any one person to wrangle. But he's never *not* been there for us, and I know as long as he's fucking breathing, he always will be.

"Kade," he says carefully, "I hope that this woman is who you think she is. I really do. I want that for you so fucking much. For all of you. But…you've got a really shitty track record. Your judgment when it comes to women is not always the best. And now? With way more zeros in your bank account, well, you're a fucking target. Just…be careful, okay?"

I want to rage at him, tell him he's wrong. That this time is different, but I swallow back my words. I've said them to him before. Last time. And the time before that.

He's not lying.

My judgment is shit.

"I will," I say tightly, wishing I'd been able to dodge this conversation longer. I'd been avoiding him as much as I could, carefully dodging the topic when I had to connect with him.

I hadn't brought Becca up with him for this very reason. Because he is wrong this time. Becca isn't like the others. She hasn't even asked me about her fucking car. That's got to mean that she doesn't care about the money. She almost walked away from me when she found out how rich I was.

I've seen women put on an act before. Fuck, I watched my mom do it when I was a kid. I can tell when I'm being played. And I don't see Becca putting on an act with me. No. Ransom is wrong this time. Becca is exactly who she says she is. And she's with me because she really likes me. I know her.

But as I head for my truck to pick up Becca, I can't quiet that little niggling worry at the back of my mind, telling me that maybe I am wrong. Maybe she's just a really excellent actress.

22

KADE

I'm relieved when I pull up to the Dojo and see Becca exiting with a group of women. I hate the idea of her walking back to the shop by herself, and I was worried the whole drive over that she'd leave without me.

She smiles as she sees me and jogs to the truck. I lean over and push her door open, knowing it's pointless to jump out and try to open it. Her smile cuts through all the bullshit in my head. It's fucking sunshine. The day that piece-of-shit car died at my garage is the luckiest fucking day of my life. Everything about my life is better with her in it.

Everything.

"Hi!" she says as she hops in. She drops her bag on the floor and leans over the center console, her lips meeting mine. I grab the back of her head and pull her in tighter to me. I love the way she smells after working out. The musk and warmth of her skin better than any perfume she could ever wear.

I'm fucking desperate to get my nose next to her skin. All of her skin. I want to know how she smells behind her knees, the crease of her thigh. I want to know how the taste of her pussy changes after a workout. I really regret ever agreeing to this stupid plan to wait. Who fucking cares if I'm her boss? There's no reason to wait anymore.

Becca draws away, her lips millimeters from mine. I tighten my grip to make sure she can't get away from me. "Jesus, Kade." She's panting, and I'm distracted watching her breasts heave in the low neckline of her top. I'm pretty sure I can get them out of there in a couple of seconds. The windows of the truck are tinted, so I doubt anyone would see. I slide my free hand from her ass up her side to her breast. Her fingers cover mine, and her laughter breaks my focus.

"Kade!"

I drag my eyes away from that spectacular rack to her face. "Huh?"

Her face is creased with laughter, and I sit back, loving the way her eyes crinkle up, making the freckles on her nose dance. She brings her hands up to cup my cheeks. "I said we can't do this here." I'm completely blank, and she takes pity on me. "We have an audience, Kade."

I shift my eyes to the front of the building, and yep, there's a group of women watching us, Holly among them. When they see me looking, they start clapping and yelling. I feel my ears getting hot, and I shake my head in embarrassment.

Becca just laughs, pulling away to lower her window. "Keep walking, ladies. Nothing to see here." She waves and watches them leave in groups before turning back to me. "Alone at last," she says with a wink.

Christ, this woman is going to be the death of me. "Becca, you're fucking killing me," I admit with a groan.

"Humm. You look pretty…primed for a man on the verge of death." She laughs at my scowl.

"I need to be in you so bad. It's all I'm fucking thinking about. I can't even focus at work anymore. My hand is just not cutting it."

Her mouth flattens, but I see the twitch at the corner. "Your hand, huh?" She smiles slowly. "Do you think about me when you're holding your cock in your fist?"

I choke and have to clear my throat before I answer. "Yeah, I do."

She's going to torture me again. I can't decide if I love it or hate it when she does this. But I can't bring myself to stop her. Becca hums low in her throat and moves her hand up to her chest, tracing her finger along the edge of her V-neck top. I groan and shift in my seat, loving her teasing and hating it at the same time.

"Have some fucking mercy, please."

Her smile turns evil. "What do you think about me doing, Kade? I really want to know."

She's fucking toying with me. But I'm too horny to play. "I think about your lips wrapped around my cock. Of burying my face in your pussy and fucking you with my tongue until you come so hard you clamp down on me. Then I think about feeding every single inch of my cock into you until I'm in you so deep you won't feel right unless you're wrapped around me."

I'm fucking aching, my words a growl. Becca's eyes are hooded, her chest rising and falling with her racing breath. She's so fucking beautiful. I can't believe she's mine. That she lets me touch her. That I get her smiles and soft touches.

"I sometimes wake up at night afraid you're going to disappear," I confess.

Her eyes widen. "What? Why?"

I shrug, needing to talk, to be honest with her, but reluctant to open up. "I...I told you I hadn't had the best track record with relationships, right? Most of the women I've dated have been..." I hesitate.

"Broken," she whispers. I nod slowly, embarrassed.

"Yeah. Broken. I wanted to help them." I have to laugh at

myself. "I always want to help. And they all wanted me to, you know? They dug their nails into me and wouldn't let go. And I let them. Fuck, I craved it. And then one day, I'd wake up, and they'd be gone."

I can see the confusion on her face, but I don't want to explain it to her. She doesn't understand a love that hurts. Doesn't know what it's like to go to sleep as a kid with a handprint on her face.

It was the first fucking touch I'd gotten in a month from my mom. I remember putting my hand over it and being glad for it. That sign that my mom actually saw me that day. That she registered my existence instead of treating me like a ghost taking up space in her house.

When you're used to being ignored, anything that pierces that veil, that makes you feel seen, is welcome. But eventually, they all left. Sometimes on their own, sometimes forced out. Sometimes, I'd find them cold, stiff, eyes gazing sightlessly at the wall. Not moving, no matter how much I beg and cry for them to wake up.

"Why would they be gone?" Becca's voice is like a soft breeze, gently pushing away the memories.

My smile turns bitter. "Sometimes because they got what they wanted...money usually. Or if they got better, they didn't want to be with me anymore."

"So they're stupid." Becca's voice is dry.

A startled laugh slips out of me at her matter-of-fact delivery. How does she do that? Listen to my deepest pain, and somehow make it better? Make me want to laugh about it? I love the way she sees me. Maybe If I'm lucky, she'll look at me that way for a while longer. I don't want to think of that changing, even though I know it will.

"I'm serious, Kade. They sound like dumb bitches. Why on earth would anyone leave you?"

"Because I'm a mess, Becca."

Her snort startles me. "I'm shocked." She smiles when I look at her in surprise. "We're all a mess, Kade. Every single person on this planet. We all have baggage. We've all made mistakes. We all have things we wish we could go back and change. That's fucking life. It doesn't mean you're not worth loving."

Looking at those clear blue eyes, I could almost believe her. Almost believe there's nothing wrong with me. That she sees some good in me.

Maybe it wouldn't hurt to pretend for a while. Pretend that I'm worth loving. But she doesn't know me. Not really. I know I should set her loose, let her go before she ends up stained by my darkness, but I won't. I'll selfishly hold on to her warmth for just a little bit longer.

"Kade," her voice is like a magnet, drawing me back to her. "Take me home, Kade."

I grip the wheel tighter, hoping I'm not imaging the invitation I hear in her voice. A better man would ignore that invitation. Would take her home and leave her at the door. Leave her to find someone who can be the man she deserves. A man who will put her needs first. But I've never been the better man. I lock eyes with hers.

"Spell it out, Becca."

Her smile is knowing and so fucking sinful. "Take me home, baby. I want you tonight." Her words are like a hit to the solar plexus, stealing my breath. I take a moment to breathe.

"I'm riding the edge already. You let me? I'm gonna use you up, Becca, " I warn her.

Her predatory smile sucks the breath out of my chest. "You can try."

Holy fuck. She looks dangerous and a little wild. I want to see what she can do to me. I turn on the truck and shift into drive, gunning it for the shop. Becca laughs and laces her fingers with mine, bringing my knuckles to her mouth. Her tongue darts out, licking my skin, making me forget my fucking name.

I can barely breathe as we swing into the driveway, and my headlights land on the figure of a woman sitting against the door to the office. I recognize the blonde hair and fancy clothes, even after all this time, and I close my eyes.

My whispered, "Fuck," comes from the very bottom of my gut. I hope that it's just a bad dream and everything will be okay when I open my eyes, but it doesn't work.

It never does.

Not when I was sitting next to my mom's body.

Not when I was lying in the hospital bed after being stabbed.

It never works.

"Who's that?" Becca asks.

"Give me a minute, please," I say, hopping out of the running truck. I take a deep breath before walking over to the woman and squatting down, all my plans for tonight fading away. "Victoria."

She doesn't move. Flashes of white clammy flesh and vomit-covered clothes flash in front of my eyes. Please, not again. I reach out and push her hair back from her face, rubbing her cheek. She looks like she's wasted away since the last time I saw her.

"Victoria," I say louder. She moans and bats at my hand, and my heart starts again. "Victoria. Get up right now." I put my hand around her bicep and pull her up. Her arm is so fucking thin.

She resists before snorting and planting her feet under her. "So bossy, Kade," she mumbles, sagging against me. She smells. A disgusting combination of vomit, body odor, and expensive perfume. I shift my head away to avoid her stink.

"Come on, Victoria. Let's get you home." I'm so tired of this. Of her. Of this fucking pattern. I hear the door of the truck open, then close, and my skin crawls. I don't want Becca seeing this. Seeing HER.

"Kade, what's going on?" Her voice is soft, hesitant.

I swallow past the lump in my throat. "Nothing you need to worry about. I'm sorry." I need to get her away from Victoria. "You should head up to the apartment. I'll see you tomorrow." I can't look at her. I don't want to see the judgment and disappointment I know will be on her face.

The light from the headlights shifts and flickers, and she walks around me to Victoria's side, reaching to take her other arm. Becca's hands look so strong and capable against Victoria's pale skin. I hate that she's being exposed to this. To my fucked up past.

"Are you going to call her a cab?" Becca's voice is hopeful. I should say yes, but I know I won't. Even now, after everything she did to me, I just can't just wash my hands of Victoria. I know I should. I know she's not my problem anymore. In my head, at least.

"I need to take her home. Make sure she gets there safely."

Becca studies me, then bites her lip and nods. "Of course you do." Her words are soft and too knowing.

We don't speak as we head to the truck. Becca opens the door and grabs her bag out as I lift Victoria and buckle her small form in the passenger seat.

She's got to be under a hundred pounds now. I've never seen her this bad. She's fucking wasting away. Clearly, rehab didn't take. The contrast between Becca's lush, healthy body and Victoria's wasted one is glaring. I wonder again what the hell I was thinking, getting involved with Vic.

I slam the door, angry at Victoria and at the fact that Becca's witnessing this fucking trainwreck. But maybe it's better she sees the truth of it. Sees exactly the type of woman that wants me.

"Goodnight, Becca." I swallow thickly, glancing at her

standing there alone in the driveway. "Lock your door, okay?" She nods, her eyes glistening in the moonlight.

"Will you come back here after?" she asks hopefully.

I shake my head no.

I'll be sitting on the bathroom floor in Victoria's apartment, making sure she doesn't choke to death on her own vomit, keeping myself awake by tracing the black veining in the marble tiles. It's a place I've spent too many nights.

"No. I'll see you tomorrow. I'm sorry, Becca." I'm so, so sorry. She stands, her eyes shifting between me and the addict in the truck. I see it then. The moment I've been dreading. The moment she looks at me like she doesn't even know me. I was right.

It's fucking devastating.

She smiles weakly and murmurs goodnight before turning and heading around the building.

I follow her to the back, waiting for her to close the apartment door before heading back to the truck. Victoria is slumped in the cab, but her eyes are open.

"Missed you, baby," she slurs.

Baby.

That word coming out of Becca's mouth just a short while ago was a promise. From Victoria's mouth, it's a lie. She always called me baby when she was high.

Baby, please, I'll change.

Baby, please don't go.

I hate that fucking word coming out of her mouth.

Vic is awake enough to complain when I get her back to her apartment. The doorman nods a hello and calls the elevator for me.

Joe. That's his name. He took me for fifty bucks one night. I came down to escape Victoria's fucking viciousness, and we spent a few hours shooting the shit and playing poker. Nice guy. Family man. He's probably got a nice wife waiting out there for him.

I wonder if she makes him breakfast in the morning? I like the idea of him getting to sit and talk with his wife over pancakes in the morning, telling her about his night. I've only seen that in fucking movies, but guys like Joe? I bet they're the ones who get it in real life.

"We'll have a little party, okay, Kade? I got some good stuff." Victoria is pawing at my hair and neck. I'm tempted to drop her so I can pry her hands off of me. I used to beg for her touch. Her attention.

Now, after Becca's sweetness, I'm fighting back nausea. I rush out of the elevator onto Vic's floor, putting in the door code to unlock it. It's still her fucking birthday. I begged her to change it to something harder to guess, but she didn't give a fuck about anything, especially her own safety.

I put her on the sofa, then back away, turning to get her a big glass of water. Her kitchen is a wreck. Dirty dishes and takeout containers litter the countertops. The garbage is rotting, and the food is dried on the dishes. She's been living like a fucking pig.

I have to laugh because no, she's been living like a fucking junkie. Pigs are cleaner than this. The counters in my apartment as a kid were just like these. Dirty dishes piled high, fucking bugs crawling on everything. Mom never seemed to care about the bugs. She never cared about anything. But I always tried to wash them, borrowing dish soap from the neighbors to try and get them truly clean. It was a losing battle most of the time. Eventually, I learned it was safer to eat straight out of the packaging.

"Where are you, baby?" Vic calls from the living room. I exhale and look in her nearly empty fridge, finding a bottle of water for her. I take it into the living room.

She's sitting up on the couch, running her fingers through her bleached blonde hair. The roots are dark. Somehow, in all of this shit, that surprises me. It didn't matter how high or how sick she was. She never missed her salon appointment.

Somehow that line of dark roots drives home how far gone she is. I silently pass her the water bottle, then move to stand at the end of the couch.

"You're a fucking mess, Vic," I tell her quietly. Her face flushes red, and those chapped, botoxed lips curl in anger.

"Who the fuck do you think you are, Kade? I look this way because of you, motherfucker." Spit is flying in her anger, and I step back out of range.

"Me? The fuck? We're not together anymore, Vic. You cheated on me and kicked me to the fucking curb, remember?"

"He was better to me than you were, Kade. He was a better man." The words shouldn't hurt anymore, considering where she is right now.

But they do.

"Yeah, that's what you said then. What happened to this fucking god of a man then Victoria? Where is he now?"

Her eyes shift away, and I know.

"He fucking OD'd, didn't he, Vic?" She nods. "When?"

"I dunno. Last week maybe?" Maybe? She doesn't even know. Jesus.

"You were clean, Victoria!" My voice is raspy. I'm so sick of this. "Why the fuck would you do this to yourself again? Why couldn't you have just stayed away from that shit? I tried so hard to help you!"

She laughs, the sound painfully rusty. "You're so fucking stupid, Kade. I wanted you gone because you wouldn't fucking stop trying to fix me. You turned into a fucking nurse, sucking all the fun out of life. I just want to live my life!" she yells. I shake my head. I swear my ears must be deceiving me.

"You're telling me that this," I wave at her pasty, frail body, "is living?"

"It's way fucking better than living with your sick ass," she sneers.

I can't even fucking look at her. "I'm not the sick one here,

Vic. You are. You're a fucking shell of a person right now. You keep this up, you'll be dead in a week."

She cackles, throwing her head back, the sound piercing through me like blades.

"You don't even know how sick you are, do you?" she says, as if I hadn't spoken. "Oh god, it's too good!" I don't want to listen to another word out of her lying mouth, but I can't make my legs walk away. "You have fucking mommy issues, Kade. Every single woman you've dated is just a replacement for her. You're trying to fix us. Make us love you the way your poor dead mommy never did." She snorts and tips sideways, burying her head in the cushions. "You'll never keep a woman, Kade. Because you're fucking broken."

I stand there, unmoving, her words twisting through my chest, nicking and slicing as they careen around. The sound of Victoria's gasping snores fills the space between us. She's going to choke if I leave her like that.

I move to shift the pillows under her mechanically, making sure she can breathe. Huh. I hold my hands up in front of me, surprised they're shaking.

I want to leave. Just walk out of this apartment, head down the elevator, and never look back. Never think of her again. But I can't. Not a fucking chance I'll sleep tonight wondering if she's lying here dead. No matter how toxic she is. So I put my back against her front door and slide down till my ass hits the floor.

Her words are ringing through my head. I want to deny them. But there's a little kernel of truth there that I can't unhear.

I am broken.

I broke the first time I walked into our apartment and found my mom laying in a pool of her own vomit. I broke the day I did CPR on her the first time. Then the second. Then the third, when I was too late.

I know I have a type.

My phone lights up, and I see a text from Becca. Becca's fucking different, I remind myself. She's not an addict or a drunk. She doesn't lie and cheat.

But I'm still the same person I've always been. I expect the worst. I'm always looking for it. I know if I look hard enough, I'll find it. Becca is too fucking good for me. She's going to end up sick of me and kick me to the fucking curb too.

23

KADE

I pull into the Knight Street Garage lot at 5:00 PM sharp. What an exhausting twenty-four hours. Victoria didn't breathe normally till sunrise. I sat, watching her the whole fucking night. Stuck with my own thoughts for company. When I finally left, I had just enough time to run home and shower before heading to the office.

Becca's last text came through at midnight. *Are you okay?*

I didn't know how to answer it.

No, I'm not okay. I don't know that I've ever been okay. The situation I'm sitting in is not okay. But it's my own fucking creation. I brought it on myself. My head is fucked. I must have written and erased twenty different replies before settling on. *I'm okay. Sorry.*

And I really fucking am. I let Victoria's shit worm its way into me. I can feel her words battering away at the already broken pieces of me. I'm waffling between trying to hold on to Becca tighter and letting her go for her own good.

I smile through the windshield when I see Becca and Holly laughing at the desk. Those two are hell on wheels together. Watching how Becca pulls Holly out of her shell makes me so fucking proud of her. She's one of the smartest women I've ever met. Not just book smart, but people smart. She seems to know when someone's soft underbelly is showing, and instead of attacking it, she works to build them back up.

I'm not used to it. Where I grew up, showing any vulnerability was a surefire way to become a victim. There was always someone bigger and badder than you, ready to tear you apart. She's so good. Too good for me.

Colton's amused voice interrupted my thoughts. "We going in, dipshit?"

"Eat shit, man."

He laughs and grabs the door handle, but I stop him with a question that's been on my mind this week. "You ever wish we had a normal childhood, man? Do you think life might have been a fuck of a lot easier? Not so much shit to navigate, you know?"

Colt slowly draws his hand back. "We're going there, huh?" He exhales heavily. "Sometimes I think about it. It's normal to wonder. But look where the fuck we are now, brother. Look at who we are. I wouldn't change a fucking thing."

"You really wouldn't change anything? Really?" I don't think I could say the same.

"You don't have to believe it, man. It's the truth. What would you change? Your mom not OD'ing?"

He's going straight for the jugular.

"Yeah, I would," I snap. "If she hadn't died, I wouldn't be such a fuckup. I wouldn't have picked such toxic relationships or gone through most of this shit."

He nods slowly. "Maybe not. But she'd still be an addict. And you'd probably be dead or in jail. We can play the what-if game until we're fucking old and gray. Truth is, we're exactly where we're supposed to be."

"How the fuck do you know that, though?" I ask, frustrated.

He flicks a glance my way. "Because we are, brother. If we were supposed to be somewhere else, doing something else, we would be. Every experience we've had has turned us into who we are right now. For better or worse." He shifts and hops out of the truck, his weight making it rock side to side. "Move your ass, dipshit. I wanna meet your lady."

He's a big pain in my ass. But he makes a strange sort of sense.

I think.

What if this is exactly where I'm supposed to be? What if Becca and I are supposed to be together? But then that would mean I was supposed to be with Victoria too. That's a bitter fucking pill to swallow. I still don't see how any good came out of that flaming pile of shit of a relationship.

I look at Becca again through the window, tracing my eyes over her smiling face. I owe her a big fucking apology for last night.

I slide out of the truck, shoving Colt aside at the door so I can go into the office first. Becca's smile falls before a smaller, tentative one takes its place. I see forgiveness there. Acceptance.

How the fuck can she just forgive so easily? I'm such a goner over this woman. She's on my mind constantly during the day and she finds me in my dreams each night.

I pull my eyes from hers, shifting my gaze to Holly, and see the nervousness on her face. Her eyes are over my shoulder, watching Colton like he's a predator. I can almost smell her fear from here. I look back at him, wanting to watch the transformation.

Colton's done this as long as I've known him. He's one of the scariest motherfuckers on the planet with the size and skill set to back it up. He carries his massive build with confidence and no small amount of natural menace, but put him in front of a woman with fear in her eyes, and he becomes a different man.

As soon as he clocks her wide eyes, everything about him changes. I watch his shoulders round, his head duck down, and a soft smile slip over his face. He suddenly looks like a teddy bear of a man instead of the killer I know he can be. It's not a mask or a deception. It's the Colton hurt women get. It's the Colton his mom got. I look back at Holly and see her face and body relaxing. It's like fucking magic. She even gives him a small smile as I introduce him.

"Becca, Holly, this is my brother Colton." Becca is smiling her big bright smile again, and it hurts that it's for him. She moves toward him, her hand outstretched. I suddenly don't want her to touch him, especially before touching me, but I slap my inner caveman down and watch as they greet each other.

"It's so great to meet you! What brings you here, Colton?" Becca asks.

"You do," he says like he's hitting on her at a bar.

"Fucker," I cough. He shoots me the middle finger, then focuses on Becca.

"Kade asked my brother Declan to look into that chick that scammed you."

Becca's eyes widen and shift to mine in question before she looks back at Colton. "Yes. I remember he mentioned it a while ago."

Colton nods, "Dec says sorry. He got tied up with another project, and he didn't have time to work on it as quickly as he had hoped. Anyway, here." He hands her a sealed white envelope. Becca accepts it and looks at me in confusion before opening it. She gasps as she fans out what I know is thirty, one-hundred-dollar bills.

"I...Oh. I... I don't understand," she stammers. Colton smiles and shrugs like it's no big deal. For him, it probably wasn't.

"Declan tracked her down for me, and I went and got your money back," he says simply.

Becca looks suspicious. "Just like that? She just handed it over?"

Colton's smile gets bigger. "Nah, that would've been a letdown. Her man got in my face a bit. Made it a bit more fun for me." He nods at the envelope. "It's all there, plus interest."

Becca's eyes get glassy, and I nudge Colton out of the way. "Piss off," I mutter to him as I wrap an arm around my girl, taking my first full breath in almost twenty hours when she leans into me instead of pushing me away like she has every right to do after last night.

Colton's smug smile makes me want to punch him, but he moves away quickly and talks softly to Holly. They head toward the door to the garage.

"I'll grab Micah!" he yells as they walk through the door. "We'll all go to dinner tonight!"

I growl but don't argue.

I don't mind spending a bit more time with my brothers and little Holly. But for now...I walk Becca backward until I reach the window to the garage. I twist the blinds until Colton's smug face is hidden from view, then wrap my arm around Becca, caging her in.

"I missed you, and I'm really fucking sorry about last night, " I say, lowering my face into the side of her neck. I love how tall she is. I press down on her a bit, liking how she takes my weight. Accepts it. I nudge her until she turns her head so I can bury my nose in my favorite spot, right where her jaw meets her neck.

As I breathe in, her unique mix of vanilla mixed with a hint of sweat gives me an immediate hard-on. Fuck. Who am I kidding? I've been hard since we pulled up out front. It's my normal state when I'm around her..

Becca's long arms wrap around my waist, and her head rests on my shoulder like it belongs there. It feels so right there. So perfect. I wonder for a moment how I'll survive if I can't feel her wrap me up again. The idea terrifies me more than anything has in a long time. I haven't even had her, but she's already in my blood, deeper than I've ever let a girl-friend. But I can't dig her out now.

Even though she's going to shatter me, leave me bleeding when this ends.

She hums and nuzzles closer to me, her breath warming the collar of my shirt, heating my skin. I feel a gentle tickle on my cheek where her hair catches on the stubble of my jaw.

"I missed you too. And I forgive you. But…" She pauses, and I hold my breath, waiting for it. "I think we're going to need to talk about it."

I nod in agreement, my heart in my throat. I don't want to think about the outcome of that conversation, so I focus on her fingers, riding up and down my spine, the tingles spreading through my whole back. I add her soft touch to the little box in my mind.

I'm saving them, all these touches. I'll pull them out and remember her when this breaks. I'll remember the way she grabbed my arm when we watched that stupid low-budget horror movie. How she'd trace the outline of my hand, running her fingers along the lines and into the dips while she tells me about her day. How she ran her fingers over the stubble on my jaw, rubbing and smoothing, looking at me like she can see right through me.

I clear my throat, "How's Holly doing?" I ask, changing the subject. "She picking everything up okay?" I want her to say no, that she needs more training. That we can rewind our ticking clock.

"She's amazing, Kade. I'm so glad she took the job. She's perfect."

Fuck.

"And Micah? Has that settled down?"

Becca snorts and tightens her arms around me. "Not, really. I still don't get it. I thought they'd be okay after their first meeting. I think he even liked her. But he's still acting like a shit. He's still scowling at her." She shakes her head in confusion. "Anyway, Holly's figured out how to deal with him. She's scowling back." She laughs. "She even wagged her finger at him yesterday. It was so funny, Kade. This little five-foot woman shaking her finger a foot above her head, right in Micah's face." She's snorting now. "You should have seen the look on his face! He has no idea what to do with her."

It's my turn to snort. "Nah, he knows exactly what he wants to do with her. And what positions. He's just fucking terrified to make a move."

Becca rears back in my arms, her eyes wide. "NO! Seriously? Micah's got the hots for Holly? I thought…maybe that first day, but then everything changed." Her hands slap on my biceps. "Oh, my god! Well, now I have to replay every moment they've ever been together in my head!"

I grin and shake my head. "How the fuck did you miss that? You spend all day with them, Becca."

She growls playfully and squeezes my arms. "I've been a little distracted, dude." She licks her lips and pushes closer, taking my breath, her lips closing in on mine. "Thinking of you."

I'm lost in her, in her soft hair and even softer mouth. My focus narrows in on her, the sounds of guys packing up in the garage fading. I tighten my arms around her lush frame, pulling her deeper into me, trapping her mouth with mine. I want all of her. I feel greedy, wanting more. Wanting everything. Like I have to get my fill now before she slips through my fingers. My hands race down her back, gripping and shaping. Her moans and restless hands. Pulling and pushing.

We ignite.

I want to push her against the wall. I want to strip off those leggings, leaving them bunched around her ankles. I want to sink into her. To disappear in her. To lose myself in the fantasy of us. In the fantasy of forever.

Colton's loud voice echoing from the back breaks into my haze, and I pull myself away from her. My lungs heaving, breaths sawing in and out. I feel wrecked. Becca's ragged breathing pierces through my fog. Her chest is heaving, nearly spilling out of the V of her shirt. I step toward her before yanking myself back, leaning against the wall.

"Dinner. Friends," I force out.

The haze slowly fades from her face, and she nods. "Right. Dinner. Holy hell, Kade." Her dazed smile chases away some of my cold spots.

When she smiles like that, I can almost imagine that everything will be okay. That our conversation will be fine, and things can stay exactly like this. But I don't really believe it. I tear my gaze away from hers and mutter. "I'll go grab them." I slip around her careful not to touch her. Her smile falls from her face, and I know it's my fault. I yank open the door to the garage, letting it bang closed behind me.

As I head toward the group huddled around Micah's bay, I'm grateful for the dinner plan and my interfering friend. I'll do whatever it takes to avoid the confrontation I feel coming.

24

BECCA

He's pulling away from me. I'm holding out hope, but it's fading. The way he watches me like he's looking for my flaws is getting to me. I find myself more and more on edge when we're together. Hell, I'm afraid to have more than one drink in front of him, worried about what I'll say. What he'll think.

It feels like he's just looking for an excuse to end things. Even when we touch.

I shake off my heavy thoughts, determined to have a good night at dinner. I'm going to be watching Holly and Micah like a hawk. I'm determined to have fun.

I don't have a mirror, but I can imagine how mussed I am. I rub my fingers over my reddened cheeks, then smooth my hair and clothes as I head toward the front window and close the blinds. I'm startled by the man who darts in the front door, his hair sticking up. There was no one out there when I looked a second ago. He's sweaty, and his eyes are darting around the office. The hairs on the back of my neck stand straight up.

I'm immediately on edge. Something about this, about him, is wrong. He's pacing back and forth, mumbling. I briefly consider heading out the front door as he paces back toward the reception desk. But no, I don't want him out of my sight. My friends are in the back, and I don't like the looks of him.

Instead, I take a long step back, putting the coffee table between us, drawing him toward me and away from the door to the bays. I catalog him as I move. An inch or two taller than me, jacket too warm for the day, T-shirt, blue jeans. Broad shoulders, straight nose. Carries himself with confidence. This man is physically dominant, used to using his strength and size. His face is tight, angry. He's on edge. He turns and locks the front door, then darts forward, and I step back again, moving so my back is to the wall. He's between me and both doors.

I hate that I'm cornered and that I let him block my exit, but I'm satisfied that he's focusing on me.

"Where is she?" His voice is hard, deep. His lips are curled up in a snarl, and his hands are balled into fists.

"Who?" I ask, but I have a sinking feeling I know exactly who he's looking for.

"My fucking wife, you stupid bitch. Where is she?" The spit flies out of his mouth, landing on the coffee table separating us. His emotions are pinging all over the place, and my adrenaline pumps. This situation is going to go to shit pretty quickly. I know it.

"I'm sorry, I don't know who you're talking about." I say, trying to slow this down. But I do know.

"My fucking wife. Where the fuck is Hannah?" he seethes.

"I'm sorry, I can't help you. I don't know anyone named Hannah. You need to leave now." I take a step toward him, pointing at the door. My voice is clear. Authoritative. Just like I've practiced my whole life. I didn't think it would work, and it doesn't. He's way too amped up.

But the red blinking lights in the corners of the room tell me the cameras are recording. It needs to be clear and on tape that I asked him to leave. I can't hear anything from the back. The bays are closed up tight already, and I don't hear voices. Maybe they're at the far end, away from the office. That thought brings me some peace. Holly's safe with the guys. And they all need to stay as far from this office as possible until this is over.

"GIVE ME MY WIFE, CUNT. YOU KNOW EXACTLY WHO I'M TALKING ABOUT!"

He reaches into the back of his pants, under his coat, and I tense. Some of my tension seeps away as I see the large hunting knife he pulls out. I can handle a knife. As long as he's over there, he can't hurt me.

And if he comes closer? Well then, I won't be the one hurting.

I have absolutely no doubt about my ability to handle him. But my tension comes right back as I hear voices approaching the door to the garage. He steps back, looking between me and the door in expectation.

Crap.

Things just got so much more complicated.

25

KADE

I make it two steps into the office, then freeze at the scene in front of me. Holly bumps into my back and I hear her strangled gasp as she moves away. I risk a glance back and see her bloodless face, eyes wide and terrified.

Micah's hands come up and ease her behind him. We lock eyes briefly before I shift them to Colton a few steps into the bay, out of view of the office. I shift so he can see my chest and sign 'knife.' He nods sharply, then silently moves back.

I turn back, focusing on the piece of shit ranting in front of me. Watching him wave that knife near Becca kills me. There's no way I'll survive losing her.

No way.

All the other women fade away, and I finally fucking see it. She's it for me. And if this goes sideways? If that knife ends up in her precious body? She'll never know how much I love her. Why the fuck didn't I get my head out of my ass sooner and tell her?

"You fucking whore, Hannah! You're such a stupid bitch." He's pacing back and forth, waving the knife in front of him, trying to get a glimpse of Holly. "Did you really think I wouldn't find your fat ass? I'll always find you. You are MINE!"

I don't spare a glance at Holly. Hannah. I'm not worried about her. Micah's a born fighter and a big motherfucker. There's no way this piece of shit is getting anywhere near Holly. Becca though? All he has to do to get to her is hop over the flimsy fucking coffee table in the way, and he's got her.

I want him away from Becca. I want her behind me.

Safe.

In all the ways I pictured losing her, I never pictured this.

Holly's chant "no, no, no," and Micah's "shhhhh" echo through my head. The lack of expression on Becca's face scares me. She's motionless, her body still, her hands relaxed at her side. The only thing moving is her eyes following the man's erratic movements.

"Becca. Come here." She glances at me and smiles before shaking her head and looking back at the man. She didn't even fucking try to come to me. Why the hell wouldn't she get to safety? She shouldn't be anywhere near this kind of danger. The man is more frantic now, his anger rising, his arms waving.

I can see his white, bloodless fingers wrapped around the knife. Behind him, through the outside door, I get a glimpse of Colton's head, crouched down. Becca's head tips slightly, her eyes glancing out the door before locking back on the man's. She's still so fucking calm it's terrifying.

"Holly, tell me what's happening," I ask. She's sobbing, and I have to resist the urge to scream at her. I need fucking answers.

"B…Brent. That's Brent. My husband," she finally chokes out. I can barely hear her over Brent's ranting.

"Brent. Brent!" I yell, stopping his pacing. "What the fuck do you think you're doing, man?" I'm trying to stay calm, but I'm pretty sure my tone is conveying a whole lot of 'I want to tear your throat out.' He spits at me, sneering.

"Collecting my property dickhead. Give me my wife."

Micah's cold voice fills the room. "No…Chance."

"You heard my brother, Brent." I say coldly. "That's not going to happen. It's pretty clear Holly doesn't want to go with you."

"HANNAH. HER FUCKING NAME IS HANNAH! SHE'S MINE. YOU OWE ME, YOU FUCKING BITCH."

I see what little control, what little reason he had slipping. My body goes cold, all my muscles twitching. This is not good. I silently beg Becca to look at me, but she's still locked in on Brent. Why is she so fucking calm?

I try to reason with Brent again, "Man, you're never going to convince us to give you Holly. There is no scenario in which you walk out of here with her. None. Your only play is to leave. Now."

The smile that curls his mouth sends a chill up my back and makes my muscles twitch. It's the same look the dealer trying to move in on our block had before he stabbed me all those years ago. I'd give anything in this moment to be the one to take the knife. It would be easier to live through that than watching another woman I love be taken away.

Suddenly, before I can even take a breath, Brent kicks the coffee table away and lunges at Becca. It feels like I'm watching a movie in slow motion. I see the magazines fly off the table. I hear the crack as the table snaps against the reception desk. I feel my heart stop as his knife arrows toward Becca.

I have a less than a millisecond to register the calm, composed look on her face, then watch in total fucking shock as her right arm sweeps out, knocking the path of the knife sideways as her hand grips his left wrist. Her body shifts sideways, her left knee rising high in front of her chest. Then she stomps it down straight through Brent's knee, cracking and breaking it until it looks like some backward robot leg from a sci-fi movie.

What the fuck just happened?

Who the fuck is she?

Her other hand joins the one on his wrist, and she steps again, dipping under his arm, her back to his front. His elbow is over her shoulder. His arm and the knife still gripped in his hand are extended in front of her. His screams of pain, already loud, reach a new pitch as she snaps her arms down toward her stomach, breaking his arm at the elbow.

Her left hand slides the knife out of his now limp hand as she turns, flowing easily to drive her right elbow powerfully into his face. Once. Twice. The blood spurts and his screaming stops suddenly, his body falling broken to the floor as Becca steps away from him. I barely register Colt's gigantic body diving through the doors or the glass spraying through the air. My eyes are locked on Becca.

Colton rolls to a stop, rising to a crouch, taking in the unconscious, bloody man on the floor and the fucking Amazon standing calmly next to him. He whistles low through his teeth before looking up at her. "Badass Becca." He raises his hand, placing it on his chest like a knight in a fucking movie. "Would you marry me?"

26

BECCA

I'm breathing through the adrenaline crash, letting it wash over me like a wave. I can almost feel the warmth of Dad's body, the circles he'd rub on my shoulders after a fight, helping me through the shakes. *Let it flow Becca, just let it flow.* They were only competitions, but the human body doesn't understand that there are referees and rules. It fires and fights like the danger is real and leaves us all shuddering at the end.

I glance at the doorway again. Kade's eyes are wide on mine. He's just staring, his face blank. Behind him, Micah is smiling. I see Holly's small hand on his arm. His arms are behind him, wrapped around her, keeping her pressed safely to his back.

Colton is still crouched in front of me. My heart stutters for a second at what I see in his eyes. The heat. The fascination. The want. He's acting like it's a joke, but I know on a gut level that if I said yes, this man would have me in front of a judge within the hour. I've seen that look before. In the eyes of the men I'd teach. The men I'd pin. The men I'd beat at every tournament I went to. The men who are not just drawn to strong women but who crave them. I let myself soak up his warmth, his obvious admiration, before reaching out to ruffle the hair at the top of his head.

"Get up, big guy. I'm taken." I wink to soften my words.

I see the regret pass over his face before the joker comes back. "Are you sure? I've been told I have a really talented tongue. I'm happy to give you a demonstration."

I laugh and shake my head, waiting for Kade to curse him out and claim me. I hear Micah laughing, but I reel back when I meet Kade's frigid eyes. He's silent and still, carved out of stone.

I barely notice Colton moving to take the knife from my hand or Micah guiding Holly into a chair, kneeling in front of her. Or the flashing lights of the police. I'm trapped by the ice in Kade's face. We answer questions, hand over security tape, and it's all a blur.

I keep making excuses for why he hasn't come to hold me. Maybe he's in shock? Maybe he's waiting for more privacy? But why? He's wrapped me up in his arms in front of an audience before. And I really need it now. Why won't he come to me? The cold in his face keeps me from going to him. I feel shaky, and I don't think I can handle him rejecting me right now.

I shake out of my daze as Holly's trembling body hits mine. I hug her close, resting my chin on her head while she sobs. I rub her back and close my eyes, so grateful that she's safe. That everyone's safe. That I could protect them. I trained my whole life for a moment like this. A moment I honestly never thought would come.

My world was always so safe. With Dad around, I always knew I would be okay. That he would have my back. So the sparring and fighting were…fun. They were part of my job. But that sense of safety was shattered when Dad got sick.

I thought I was rebuilding that here, though. That I would have Kade in my corner. Maybe I was wrong because it suddenly feels like a fucking football field is between us. Holly's sobs taper off, and I dip my head to meet her eyes.

"You're okay, Hol."

She nods and sniffles. "I didn't see," she says, her voice thick with tears. "Did you use some of the moves you're teaching us in class?"

I smile gently and squeeze her a little tighter. "Yeah, hon, I did. And a few that are a little more advanced."

She nods, deep in thought, before firming her lips and drawing her spine up. "I want to learn those too." Her voice is firm. Sure. And I'm so proud of her.

"I'll teach you," I promise her. And I will. Every woman that walks through my self-defense class will learn how to protect themselves. But Holly? My dear friend Holly? I'm going to teach her how to make men cry if she wants me to. "Will you let Micah take you home?" I whisper to her.

She nods against my cheek.

"Micah, could you please take Holly home?" I ask. The way Micah wraps his arm around her, comforting her, is sweet. Dad would wrap me up like that while I was shaking through the adrenaline crash at a tournament. Or when that little weasel Jack asked me to the ninth-grade dance and then kissed Julia. I kept it together until Dad picked me up. Then I let go, knowing he'd hold me together until I could be strong again. He always held me through the high moments and the low. He was always so present, so solid, so safe.

I miss him.

I watch Micah and Holly get to the car, then turn as Colton stops beside me. "Badass Becca."

We smile.

"Those were some pretty killer moves."

I nod, waiting for the question I know is coming. I could tell when he walked in the door that he trained in martial arts. The fluidity in his body as he moves is a dead giveaway.

He carries himself the way the top fighters do. The way I do. With absolute confidence in themselves and their abilities.

"What kind of training have you got?"

I tap my chin. "Hummm," I say, playing with him a bit.

"Becca," he coaxes playfully, wiggling his eyebrows at me.

I drop my finger and shrug my shoulders. "Third Dan BJJ. First Dan in Tae Kwon Do. Fourth Dan in Judo," I say with a smile. Colton's eyes get wider at each belt I list off, his admiration for the years of dedication to martial arts clear.

I sneak a glance at Kade leaning on the reception desk. I don't know what I hoped to see on his face. Admiration. Love. Affection. Acceptance. Something warm. I don't find it, and it leaves me feeling colder. Colton's whistle brings my attention back to him.

"Maybe we can spar sometime, Badass Becca," he asks, golden retriever energy spilling from him. "I think we can learn a lot from each other."

"Deal," I say softly, knowing I'll make it happen. Even if things fall apart with Kade like I think they're about to. I watch Colton wave and exit out the front, hopping into the backseat of Micah's car.

I shudder, feeling the arctic blast coming from Kade, and take a deep breath before turning to meet his eyes. I miss the warmth he usually looks at me with. The little curve on the corner of his mouth as he teases me. We stand, staring at each other, and I'm terrified to speak first. Maybe I'm wrong about what he's thinking.

"This isn't going to work," he blurts.

I wait, my mouth dry, heart pounding. Hoping that he'll smile and say he's making some stupid joke. The tension between us is snapped by the glare of headlights and slamming doors outside. I glance over my shoulder and see the glass guys working to unstrap the new front door from the side of their truck.

"I'm going home. I need to shower the blood off," I

mutter, walking around him, grabbing my purse, and rushing into the bays and out the back door. I don't look back at him.

I can't.

When I was little, Dad had an old vase of his mom's on our mantle. It had little hairline cracks running throughout the white porcelain. Our house looked like a bachelor decorated it, so the vase always looked a little out of place.

But I was fascinated by the cracks. I thought they made the vase look cool. But one day, when Dad and I were goofing around, that vase came tumbling down, shattering on the wood floor. I begged him to try and fix it, but he explained to me that the vase was weak and that when something weak breaks, sometimes there's just no putting it together again.

I understand what he meant by that today, more than I ever have.

27

KADE

I lock the new front door, then slump down into a chair. What a fucking mess. Everything blew up tonight, and it's all my fucking fault. I can't bring myself to go upstairs to face her. I knew this was coming, that she'd move on, but I thought it would be because she got sick of me, not because I'm a colossal asshole.

A rap on the door startles me. I shift to see Colton's large frame outside.

"Open the door dickhead." His voice is clear, even through the thick glass door.

"What are you doing back here, man?" I ask.

"Checking on you. What else would I be doing?" Of course he is. He's incapable of minding his own fucking business.

"I'm fine. We've been through worse. You know that," I say as I open the door. Colt's belly laugh makes me want to punch him in the face. I'd do it, too, if his jaw wasn't made of fucking titanium. Last thing I need is a broken hand to go along with my broken heart.

"You're so far from fine, brother." When I don't answer, he

continues. "What the hell was that, Kade?" he asks aggressively.

"What was what?" Playing dumb hasn't ever worked with him, but it's worth a try.

"Don't play that fucking game with me, Kade. I know you too well. You froze her out. Your eyes were movie-villain cold." Colton's arms are crossed, his feet planted wide apart. No way will I be able to move this asshole. When he gets like this, a bulldozer can't move him.

I sigh, rubbing my hands on the top of my head. "You're not going to let this go, are you?"

His smile turns sad. "I can't watch you do this, man."

"Do what, Colt?"

"Destroy the best fucking thing to ever happen to you?"

I snort. "Really? What the fuck do you know about anything? You only met her tonight."

"True. But I know you. You've been a different person the last month."

"Sure." I scoff. "I'm all sun-shiny and shit?"

Colt's face is so serious. "You're fucking alive, man." I shake my head, turning to stalk behind the reception desk. "It's true, Kade. You know it is. You've been a zombie for as long as I've known you."

"Fuck off, Colt. You have no idea what you're talking about." I'm not a fucking zombie. Sure, I've been phoning it in for a while, but what does he expect from me?

"Yeah, I do, man. You've been my brother for over twenty years. I've been watching you." He exhales heavily. "You've been existing. You're there for your brothers, always. But in your own life, you're fucking drifting. All those women you let take advantage of you? There'd be a little spark in you when you first met them, then, poof, it would be gone. They'd drag you way the fuck down. And I gotta tell you, brother. I'm really pissed at you for that."

I cross my arms and raise my eyebrows. "Really? Why the fuck would you have any feeling about it?"

Colt growls, stalking toward me. I ball up my fist, wanting to shut him up but knowing I'd never hit him. At the end of the day, he's still my brother and I don't want to hurt him. Even if I could.

The toes of his boots hit mine, and he leans into me until our noses are almost touching. "You dumb motherfucker. You're my brother. I fucking love you. And anything that hurts you is not okay with me. And you hurting yourself? Really fucking not okay, Kade!" he yells.

He has no idea the shit running through my head. I don't want him to know. But he has to see. How can he not? He says he knows me? Bullshit.

"I'm fucking broken, man," I admit harshly. "I want them to get better. I thought maybe if I tried…" I drift off.

Colt nods, "I know, man. You want to make it better for them. You're always trying to fix them, but you're not going to find what you need with those women."

I sigh, too fucking tired for this. "Okay, Dr. Phil, what do I need?" Colt's thick fist comes up and raps my chest

"To fucking know that you're worth loving, man."

I raise my eyebrows at him. "Seriously, dude?" Is he fucking kidding? I don't need anything from those women. They needed me. They needed my help. Why is it so wrong to try and help people?

Colt swats my face. "Pay attention, dipshit. This is way overdue, and I want to make sure you don't miss a second of this. Since your dumb ass can't seem to connect the dots in your own fucking life, I'm going to lay it out for you. Ready?"

I growl at him, and he swats my face again. "Asshole, stop slapping me!"

He swats me again. "Not until you're fucking paying attention," he says calmly. I yell at him in frustration and drive my fists into his stomach. He barely grunts, just staring at me like I'm the dumbest fucking person on the planet.

"WHAT!" I finally shout, crossing my arms to glare at him. I'll hear him out, then kick his ass out. I'm pretty sure I still have a bottle of Jack stashed in the desk. I'll get nice and numb, then go let Becca destroy me.

"You are a good man, Kade." Colton's voice is deep. "You are always there for your brothers. You're really fucking smart. You've got the kindest heart out of all of us. And somehow, you don't see it."

"What don't I see, Colt?" I ask, avoiding his piercing eyes.

"That you fucking deserve to be loved just the way you are, man."

"Yeah, you said that already."

"But you're not really getting it, brother. Do you even realize what you were doing with all those women before Becca?" I groan and roll my eyes.

"I'm sure you'll fucking enlighten me." My sarcasm just bounces off him.

"You find the most damaged women, the fucking trainwrecks, and try to fix them up. Because you think that if you fix them, then they'll stay and love you. Only it doesn't work that way, man. They get better and leave, right? That's what you told me." I nod and crack my neck, uncomfortable with this conversation. "So they leave, and it reinforces the fucking pattern you've lived your whole life, starting with your mom."

I sigh, backing up to sit on the desk. "When I meet them, they're not fucking trainwrecks, Colt."

Colt's eyes are too knowing. "They're fuck-ups when you meet them, Kade. You just never seem to notice. You don't want to notice."

Christ. If I wanted to see a shrink, I have enough fucking money to hire one. "Where'd you get your fucking psychology degree, man?"

"At the U," he says, "Masters Thesis is almost done."

I laugh but shoot to my feet as I get a clear look at his face. "You're fucking kidding, right?"

Colt shakes his head. "Nope."

Who is this guy?

He's the head of security for Brash Corp. He's covered head to toe in tattoos, and I know for a fact he's still hitting the illegal cage fights across the tracks. And now this?

"Who the fuck are you, man? Why the fuck are you getting a degree, and why wouldn't you tell us?"

He shrugs, smiling a bit. "We're all fucked up, man. I figured it wouldn't hurt to figure out why, and what to do about it." He taps his temple with two fingers. "You don't even want to know the shit I have going on. It's all kinds of crazy up here."

I laugh in disbelief. "Crazy? You supposed to be using that word?"

He snorts and drops his hand. "Most of the professors have no idea what to do with a meathead like me. They tried to run me off at first. Fuckers didn't know who they were dealing with. I'm a fucking burr, man. They might not like the word crazy, but sometimes it just fits, ya know?"

I nod dumbly.

"Kade, I really do know what I'm talking about."

I study him. He looks so serious. I've never really seen that look on his face outside of work. I finally nod and his dark eyebrows relax slightly.

"Listen, when we're kids, our parents are the whole world, right?" he says. "Everything we understand about the world comes from them. And as little kids, we're programmed to search out affection and love. You with me so far, brother?"

I nod again, listening despite myself.

"Okay. So when a little kid is living with a drug-addicted mom who sometimes disappears on him. Doesn't always feed him enough or pick him up when he cries. It fucks up the wiring in his brain. It creates trauma-based patterns. And eventually, that kid figures they'll need to get their needs met in other ways."

"Like?" I ask, curious despite my frustration with this conversation.

"Like taking care of a shitty mom, so she'll love on him for a bit. Give him the tiniest bit of affection that he needs to survive." My mind flashes to the slaps, those little signs that she saw me.

But survival?

"Food is survival, Colt. Shelter and warmth, too. But love, man?" Maybe they'll give him a refund on all that fucking tuition he paid.

Colt shakes his head in exasperation. "You remember those stories about kids in orphanages in Eastern Europe?"

"I…maybe?" Images of rows of cribs and sunken eyes flash through my mind.

"The kids are taken in by the government, but there are not enough people working there to take care of all the kids. So their physical needs are met, but they don't get fucking cuddles, man." His voice is pained. "They don't get talked to or sung to. They don't have people looking in their eyes and smiling at them. Loving them." Colt backs up, his shoulders dropping. "It's so fucking sad, man. They waste away. It's called Failure to Thrive. A lot of the babies die. The ones that make it have permanent neurological deficits."

Where we grew up, death was commonplace. But babies wasting away in their cribs? That's a whole other level of fucked up.

"Jesus. That's fucking awful. But what does it have to do with me?" I honestly don't know where he's going with this.

"I'm just spitballing here, brother," He reaches out and taps the center of my chest. "But I wonder what would happen to a kid who learned the only way to get love is to try and make his mom better. What kind of man do you think that kid will grow up to be? What kind of woman do you think he'll be attracted to?"

I sink down to the desk again, gripping the edge tightly. The similarities between my mom and all the women I've dated flashing through my head.

Well shit.

"It sounds so fucking obvious when you say it like that," I admit.

"Yeah. Took me a lot of years to learn this shit. But once you see it, you can't unsee it," he confirms.

"So you're basically saying that I'm fucking broken, and I look for broken women so I can fix them, hoping they'll what…love me?"

"You tell me, man. When you helped them get healthy, what did you want to have happen in the relationship?" I lock my fingers behind my neck, looking down at the tile floor, flipping through the revolving door of shit that is my love life.

"I wanted them to stay with me without needing the drugs or the other guys," I admit.

"Because…" he prompts. I groan. He's going to make me say it.

"Because I would be enough for them."

"Ding, ding, ding! Give the man a prize." He's smiling, but he doesn't look happy. "You keep thinking if you fix these women, then they'll love you. And when they leave, man? Then it reinforces this subconscious belief you have that there's something about you that makes you unloveable."

"So basically, I'm broken as fuck?"

He exhales heavily. "If someone handed you a five-year-old little boy tomorrow—surprise, you have a son—would you treat him the way your mother treated you? Leave him alone in a roach-infested apartment? Starve him? Hit him?"

My stomach turns at the thought. I swallow down the acid creeping up my throat. "No fucking way. Never."

"Of course you wouldn't. Because as shitty as your childhood was, you are a good man. Your childhood damaged you some, but you're not fucking broken. You are not a pathetic excuse for a human. You broke the pattern with Becca, man. She's nothing like the women you normally go for. She's got her shit together. So get your fucking head on straight and fix it."

He throws up his hands. "That was fucking exhausting, brother!"

I have to laugh. "Oh yeah, my personal trauma tire you out?"

"Yeah," he mutters, heading to the door. "Need pie." And he's gone.

I lock the door and drop back into my chair, head spinning.

Jesus.

How did he just flip everything I thought I fucking understood about the world? What do I do next? How the hell do I fix the damage I just did with Becca? I cringe when I think about the way I reacted to this whole fucking situation. I deserve a nut punch.

But shit, why wouldn't she have run? Get to fucking safety. She has to stay safe. I don't think I'll fucking survive it if she's hurt. I can feel my pulse racing again. The fear I felt at that moment rises again, filling my body. I don't fucking understand what the hell she was thinking. How could she fucking do that to me?

———

28

BECCA

I manage to hold back the tears until I hit the door at the top of the stairs.

I'm so fucking stupid. I had hoped we were building something the last few weeks. That he truly saw me. I wanted to believe in him, in us, so badly. And then he looked at me like I was a complete stranger. I just wanted him to hug me. To know that everything was going to be okay. And he couldn't do it.

I don't try to stop the tears, letting them fall through my shower. Through pulling on my sweats and T-shirt. Through my erratic searches through the *Roommate Wanted* listings. No way am I staying here anymore.

The envelope Colton gave me is sitting on the table, a whole new world of options under its flap. I can pay to fix the car. Or I can junk it and use the cash to get a place. I'm not stuck. If I'm honest with myself, I've never been stuck. I could have left at any time. I chose to stay, and I might as well own it. I put myself in this position.

I push my fingers through my wet hair and breathe out some of the tension. Going over everything that just happened is not going to make anything better, and I'm already sick of wallowing. No more tonight. I stare at the fridge, trying to remember what I have left in there for supper. But all I remember is pickles.

The knock on the door freezes me halfway to the fridge. There's only one person who could be on the other side of that door.

I don't want to do this.

I know it's coming, but I'm not ready yet for it to be officially over. If we wait. If we avoid each other, then I can keep this little kernel of hope in me alive for just a little while longer. The second, harder knock propels me forward. I rest my forehead on the door.

"I'm exhausted, Kade. Can we skip this part?" I say softly, proud of how level my voice is.

"Open the fucking door, Becca." The anger in his voice slams into my chest, into my simmering pool of hurt and anger.

It boils over.

I swing the door open with a glare, letting it bang against the wall before turning my back and heading into the small kitchen. Kade closes the door with a soft click that makes the back of my neck tingle. This is going to be bad. I turn, facing him head-on. If he wants a fucking fight, I'll give him one.

He shoves off the door and turns to me, pushing his hands into his pockets. "What the fuck were you thinking, Becca?"

What was I thinking? Seriously? I'm too angry to fuck with him, to toy with him.

"I was thinking I need to protect the people I care about, Kade. I was thinking that I have the skills and training to keep you all safe."

The muscle in his cheek jumps. "Me, Micah, Colt, we were all there. Why didn't you let us handle it?"

"Handle it," I repeat quietly. "You wanted me to let *you* handle it?" My voice rises. "How exactly did you expect that to work, Kade? When he lunged at me with the knife, should

I have let him cut me? Stab me? Take me hostage, maybe? What exactly did you want me to do?"

He shoves his hand through his hair and growls. "You shouldn't have fucking been there, Becca! You shouldn't have been in danger in the first place. Why didn't you get out of there? You could have run out the door. I saw the footage. You had a choice when he came in. You chose not to leave. Why?" His words are running together, tumbling over each other, coming faster and faster. His questions scrape along my skin.

"I...Seriously? Do you really not understand?" What kind of person does he think I am? How could he think those things? "Why would I leave Kade? How could I leave, knowing that people I love would still be in danger? I...I am not capable of walking away from someone who needs me. Someone I can help."

His disbelief pierces me to my core, and I sit in the hurt as I watch him, rubbing his hair, eyes no longer cold. They're wild, bouncing from my face to the room and back again. A thread of understanding appears, and I tug on it, wondering where it will lead.

"You've been expecting me to leave, haven't you?" I ask him. His body stills, his eyes focusing on my feet. "You fix them up. Your mom. Those other women. Then they leave. One way or another, right?" I want his eyes on me. I'm not letting him hide from me anymore. If we're going down in flames tonight, I want to make sure we lay it all out on the table. "Kade, look at me for this conversation. You owe me that much." His eyes reluctantly rise to meet mine. I hurt, seeing the pain in his eyes. "They don't need you anymore, and they leave, right?" I ask again.

He clears his throat. "Sometimes. They...they get healthy, and I send them away. Or sometimes my brothers, Ransom, will send them away. I can't walk away if they need me."

I nod slowly, the picture becoming clearer. "So now that

I'm all 'fixed,' you're ready to send me away? That's why you froze me out?"

His emphatic "NO" is followed by a quieter, "I don't know." He pushes his hands through his hair again, looking at a spot between us on the floor. "You're not like them. Not really. I got…attached before. But nothing like this. I can't do this, Becca. What if you'd died today? I can't lose you like that. It's too much. You'll be safer if we're not together." Safer? That makes no sense. Nothing that happened tonight had to do with him. But there are no fucking guarantees in life. I wish there were.

"Kade, you are all kinds of fucked up," I say with a sad smile. His head jerks up, surprise on his face. "If you're looking for a safe relationship, you're going to be shit out of luck. You've set this up," I say, my hand waving at the space between us, "in your mind so you…we, end up alone, no matter what. I'll either go away because I don't need you anymore, or I'll go away because it might hurt to lose me? Jesus, talk about a rock and a hard place." I shake my head, baffled by his logic. "What a shitty way to live, Kade."

His mouth firms and his eyes flare. "You don't have the first fucking clue what it's like to watch someone self-destruct, Becca. It's soul-destroying."

I laugh in disbelief. Does he seriously think he's the only one who's lost someone?

"No, you're right. I don't know, dumbass. But I know exactly what it's like watching someone you love slip away," I sob, the pressure in my chest needing a release. "I watched my dad fade away, Kade. I held him as he cried on the bath-room floor. I helped him shave his head when the chemo made his hair fall out. I cleaned him up when he couldn't control his bowels at the end. I was there for every single, heartbreaking, soul-destroying second of it."

My eyes are red, my loss and pain naked on my face. He needs to see it. See that I can fucking live with it. That I wear it proudly, a sign of how much I loved my Dad. Love him still. "And you know what, Kade? I would do it all over again in a heartbeat if it meant I could have him back again, even if it was just for an hour. Being there for the people you love. It's not a burden. It's a privilege." Kade's motionless, focused on me. I wipe my eyes, so tired of all of it. The pulling away, the doubt.

"I never needed you," I tell him, honestly.

He frowns and slowly shakes his head. "Everything you own was in your car, Becca. You needed help."

I shrug, and his mouth tightens.

"You did," he insists.

"Maybe, but I had more than enough money in my wallet for a bus ticket home. I could have gone to a hostel or gotten a hotel room. And I have the names of at least ten people in this city I met through the tournament circuit who would let me crash on their couch in a heartbeat. I was in a shitty spot, Kade, yes. But I had options other than you."

I'm so tired. He's so lost. We're so lost.

"When I met you," I say quietly, "I made the choice not to exercise any of them. I wanted to be near you. And you were so insistent on helping. I let you."

I step closer to him, hating that I'm going to hurt him, but needing to give him the whole truth. "I don't need you. I don't need you now. And I didn't need you then." I press my hand briefly to his chest, wanting to feel his warmth one last time. "I chose you, Kade," I whisper before dropping my hand and moving around him toward the door, needing him to go.

29

BECCA

His hand tangling with mine, dragging me to a stop, steals my breath. I clench my eyes shut, not sure how much more of this I can take. "You were already leaving Becca," he says quietly, "You got a different job, remember."

"Yes, Kade. I remember," I say shortly. "I left the garage for a job doing exactly what I love. That didn't mean I was going to leave you. You're the one that kept pulling away."

"I know," he says, voice heavy. I squeeze his fingers briefly before relaxing in his hold. "You're nothing like them. I know that. But...it just didn't make sense why you'd want to be with me otherwise."

I can hear the weight of our mistakes in his voice. My heart is breaking all over again. How can he not see how wonderful he is? "Oh, Kade. There's so much more to you than what you can do for people. You're such an amazing friend. You're a great boss. You're kind and giving. You care about people. And you look at me, big Becca, one of the guys, Becca, like I'm a supermodel. Why wouldn't I want to be with you? But if you can't see that? If you can't believe that. There really is no hope." My voice breaks at the end. I tug on my hand, but his grip tightens.

"Colt just said the same thing," he says, his voice ragged. "He thinks you're the best thing to ever happen to me."

I feel him coming before he touches me, the waves of heat coming off his body warming my back as he approaches. I shudder as he presses his body against me, his thighs against mine, his groin to my ass.

His head lowers, and he growls in my ear, "When he came at you with that knife, Bec, fuck, that was the worst moment of my life by far."

His hands grip my arms, pulling me tighter, closer until I can't tell where he ends and I begin.

"Somehow…you became everything to me over the last month. It's fucking terrifying. So yeah, I pulled away." His hands tighten on my shoulders. "But knowing you could be taken from me in that office, in that moment…it was fucking awful. But," he pauses, clearing his throat, "you broke him, Becca. I…fuck. You had that piece of shit unconscious before I could get to you."

I tense, worried about what he's going to say next. "You were so cold, Kade. You looked at me like I was a stranger."

I feel him nod and exhale. "I'm sorry. I was…battling with myself. About not being able to protect you. About losing you. I have no idea how to handle you, Becca. You're so much more than I expected. Than I've ever had…You don't need me." His voice is tinged with wonder.

"No," I agree, hope and fear warring inside me.

"You could walk away any time," he mutters.

"Yes. I could."

And I will if I have to.

But the little spark of hope in my chest is growing. Kade's hands brush down my arms, taking my hands and squeezing them before bringing our arms up and crossing them over my chest. I'm caged in. Surrounded by him. And despite all the hurt of today, the pain, it still somehow feels like home.

"Colton came back tonight." His voice rumbles gently in my ear. "He pointed out a few things that I really fucking needed to hear. And well…I guess I'm going to have to work to keep you." My breath hitches as he continues. "I am a single-minded bastard, Becca. I will love you so good, you'll never want to leave me. I don't want to lose you, so I'll make damn sure my stupidity won't ruin this again. I'm so fucking sorry." His arms tighten as I lean into him, letting my tears spill over.

"Love?" I ask around the lump in my throat. That hope grows a little bigger, but with it comes fear. Fear that he'll find another reason to leave.

"I love you so fucking much. More than I ever thought possible," he whispers, rocking me slowly until the torrent of tears turns to a drizzle.

"Do you think you can forgive me?" he asks hesitantly. I inhale and exhale deeply, focusing on the doorknob.

Can I forgive him?

"You keep pushing me away. You're always looking for the bad, Kade," I say thickly.

He nods, his jaw rubbing on my temple, but lets me continue.

"I don't want to be in a relationship like that. I need someone who's on my side, not someone looking for my weaknesses. I…I can't always feel like I have to be on guard with you, waiting for you to flip out."

His breath hitches, and he tries to turn me in his arms. I resist, gripping his hands tighter. I can't look at him during this conversation. It's too much.

"I can be that man, Becca. I am on your side. I fucking swear it," he says firmly. "I will do whatever I have to do to make this right. To get my head fucking straight." I hear how sure he is. But I thought he was sure before. I take another deep breath and let it out.

"This won't happen again, Kade," I tell him calmly. "If you pull this shit again, if you push me away again, I'm done. I won't allow you to treat me that way. I don't care how much I love you. I'll walk."

His arms tighten reflexively when I say the word "love." Does he not know? How could he not? I thought I was giving off those dumb woman-in-love pheromones or something. He curls me into him even tighter, his head pressing against mine. His lips rest at the corner of my mouth.

"You're the best person I know," he says raggedly. "If I'm spinning out, I promise I'll talk to you or to Colton until I have my head on straight. I will never give you a reason to doubt me again. I will never put my shit on you again. I am yours, Becca, completely."

I let his words settle into my bones. The certainty in them soothing the hurt.

I can't know what the future holds, and honestly, I'd rather be surprised, but if I have my way, there will be a whole lot of Kade in it.

But I was telling the truth. I won't allow this to happen again, to become some toxic pattern in our lives. Sometimes leaving is the smartest thing you can do. And I'm a very smart woman.

We stand, pressed together, slowly rocking away the hurt. I turn my head slightly, soaking in the soft kisses Kade's pressing to my face. His voice finally breaks the peaceful silence. "Why didn't you tell me you were a fucking ninja?"

I laugh and turn in his hold, wrapping my arms around his waist, meeting his warm eyes. "Ninja? Seriously?"

"You kicked his ass without breaking a sweat, Becca. How did I not know you could do that?"

I shake my head, baffled. "I told you I grew up in a Dojo. That I'm working in one now. I teach self-defense, Kade." I have to laugh. This man. How can he be so oblivious? I raise up on my tiptoes, lining up our mouths. "Kade," I breathe, "I'm a fucking ninja."

I swallow his laughter as I press my mouth to his. His arms are tight bands around me, running up and down my back. His kiss is urgent, fierce. Like nothing I've ever felt before. He feels different.

We feel different.

Like the veil that was between us, keeping us apart, has been torn away. This is what I wanted. His passion, his single-minded focus. His love. For the first time, I feel like I can touch him the way I've wanted to.

I run my hands up under his shirt, sliding it up as I go. I yank my mouth away from his, and he groans in protest. The groan turns to a moan as I press my mouth to his stomach, traveling up along the line of dark hair, up toward his nipples. He's powerful with his clothes on.

But underneath?

Well, Thor has nothing on him.

And he's all mine. I can't resist licking and biting those dark nipples, and his shudder sends little bolts of lightning to my pussy. His hands fist in my hair while I taste him, adding a bite to the experience that has me flushed. Kade pulls me up, tucking his head in my neck.

"You're so fucking perfect. Your taste…fuck I want all of you." His frantic words are muffled on the skin of my neck.

Yes. Yes. All I can think is yes. I want everything. I want all of him.

I gasp as I feel my bare feet leave the cold, worn linoleum floor. My wet hair swings and slides against Kade's arms wrapped tight around my back as he carries me toward the bed. I take a moment to marvel at his strength, at the ease with which he's carrying me.

He didn't even grunt. Like, not even a little one.

Something about him picking me up is so freaking hot it shoots my need to a hundred.

My stomach clenches in anticipation of having that strong chiseled body pressing me down, pushing, thrusting. Serving me. I want to leave him wrecked. I got fucking robbed last night. He needs to make it up to me now.

Then, the coolness of the sheet is against my back, Kade's firm hands pulling and yanking off my shirt, nearly tearing my bra off.

We're both urgent, panicked. It feels like we're on a runaway train, and absolutely nothing will stop us this time. It better not. If he pulls away, I will literally murder him. I'm gasping, clenching my fingers on his T-shirt, dragging it over his head, our mouths parting reluctantly before clashing together again.

I can't breathe.

I don't care.

Kade tears his mouth from mine. "Christ, you smell so good. I want more. I can't believe you're mine. I've been hard as a fucking rock since the day I met you."

His mouth is nipping, sucking, licking. I can't think, the sensation making my legs clench, my hands grasping at his hair. I lose my grip as his fingers slide under the waistband of my sweats and panties, yanking them down and off my bare feet. The cool air tickles across my wet folds and soft curls. Then he's there, pushing between my legs. I feel the material of his dress pants brushing over me, the fly pressing into me.

I groan in frustration at the sensation and bark at him, "Kade, take your fucking pants off. NOW."

He hums and pulls away, panting. His face is dazed as he stares down at me, his eyes running over my wet nipples, down my soft stomach, stopping on my pussy, open and exposed to him. Snarling, he dives toward me. I squeak, snapping my legs shut and shoving him in the chest with both feet.

"PANTS! NOW! You can't have it until you get naked, Kade."

His eyes sharpen, and he focuses back on me, shaking off his daze.

"Fuck. Pants." He wastes no time, desperately stripping off the rest of his clothes. As he shoves down his pants and underwear, I get my first look at all of him. The way he's panting is making all his muscles bunch and flex, his cock slapping against his stomach. I press my legs even tighter together to ease the ache, but it doesn't help. The only thing that will fix it is getting that big cock in me.

His muffled cursing as he dances around trying to untangle his pants makes me giggle. This man is so gone for me, so frantic for me he's completely lost his cool. There's something so heady about having this powerful man burning for me. He's like a completely different person than the man I met outside the garage that night.

He's not cold anymore.

Kade finally kicks his pants across the room, then roughly grasps my ankles, yanking my legs apart as he fits himself between them again. I make him work for it. Earn it. Thrilled when he overpowers me.

I want so much.

I want his head between my thighs, his mouth drinking me up, making me scream. But we're too wild. Too needy. I'm a little bit afraid that this is a dream. That if we wait any longer he'll disappear and I'll be left alone, empty and aching.

I feel the heat of him sliding through my pussy lips as he lowers to me, threading his hands under my shoulders, his mouth pressing to mine. His hips shift, seeking until he lines us up.

Suddenly he yanks his mouth away.

"Fuck. Condom." He pushes up away from me, but I wrap my strong legs around his, pinning him to me.

"I'm on the pill."

His eyes search mine before a slow smile spreads across his face. There's no more stopping after that. No more giggles. Kade shifts to his elbows, pressing his chest against mine. The rasp of his chest hair over my nipples makes me pant. He shifts back, sucking my nipple into his mouth, the deep pulls making my pussy cramp. My legs are restless, my feet rubbing up and down the back of his thighs. He pulls away, making me whine in frustration. Reaching down, he runs his fingers through my soaked lips, humming as he strums my clit.

"Don't you fucking dare." I gasp. "I'm already on edge. I want you!"

He chuckles darkly but obeys. Smart man. I feel the head of his cock pressing against me, once, twice. He's not small, and it's been a long time, but on the third push, I let him in. We moan together when he's all the way in, his pubic bone pushing against my clit. I wrap my legs around him again and reach down to dig my short nails into his fabulous ass. I'm not strong enough to control him in this position, but he gets the point.

He takes my lips with his, but we're both too wrapped up to maintain a kiss. Instead, our mouths are pressing together as we pant and moan. There's so much heat. Our bodies are slick with sweat. It's everything I hoped it would be.

He's everything I hoped he would be.

And judging by the noises he's making, I'm fucking blowing his mind.

He's a workhorse, driving into me over and over until I combust. He holds me, still moving gently as I ride the waves, clenching around him. I relax my fingers, pretty sure I left some nasty marks on his ass. I wrap my arms around his shoulders, pulling him tighter into me.

"Now you. Now, Kade, now."

He shakes his head, "Not yet. You're so beautiful, baby. I need you to come again. Together, baby, we're fire."

No way am I going to disappoint him, so I tighten my arms around him and widen my legs, feeling the stretch in my inner thighs. Might as well give him more room to work.

And work he does.

Until nothing exists but the two of us, and I'm screaming his name. Only then, as my shudders subside, does he finally let go, his thrusts becoming harder, more erratic.

"I love you, I love you, I love you," he groans as he comes, his hips slowing, riding out the high.

As our breathing slows, he pulls out with a bite to my neck. He gathers me up, tucking me under him, safe, sheltered.

Kade's running soft kisses across my face, my eyelids, down my jaw. "I never knew," he whispers between kisses. "I didn't know it could be like this, Becca."

I hum in agreement and slap his shoulder. "Just think what you've been missing! We could have been doing this the whole time, asshole."

His chuckle rumbles through me, but he pulls his head back to look at me, his smile slowly slipping away as he shakes his head. "No, baby. It wouldn't have been like this."

His fingers are gently rubbing my cheekbone. His focus moved inward for a moment before coming back to me. His eyes are a little lost. A little sad. I wish I could wipe it all away for him, but I can't. I don't want to. I love the man he is, so maybe I have to love everything that made him who he is now.

Even the painful stuff.

Kade's fingers travel up, tracing my eyebrows, feathering my eyelashes. Having a man so hard touch me so gently is just...everything.

"I wasn't ready for you, Becca," he admits. "I knew you were different...but I didn't realize I could be, too." He sighs, dipping in to rub his nose along my cheek. "I'm so sorry it took me so long. I'm sorry I hurt you."

He'd apologized before, but here, in the peace after the storm, his words feel deeper. Truer. I let them sink deep, through my skin and muscle, until they settle there, right in the middle of my chest. I smile up at him, ready to move on. To let the defenses, the protections around my heart, go.

I thread my hands through his hair. "I know. It's over now. I accept your apology." My nose crinkles as my smile gets bigger. "It's time for amends," I say as I press on the top of his head, pushing him down my body.

Kade's smile matches mine as he slides down between my legs, his wide shoulders spreading my thighs. "It might take me a while. I've got a lot of fucking amends to make."

"Take your time," I murmur, letting myself slide into the feel of him. Of us.

We feel fucking amazing.

30

BECCA

"Well, shit."

Somehow even though I know Kade is a freaking billionaire, I didn't expect this. There are a lot of high-rises in this city, admittedly this one is one of the nicest. Driving into the underground lot and going through an extra security gate to the private parking area gave me a hint. But it was the private elevator with handprint security that really drove the point home.

Becca, you're not in Kansas anymore.

Kade's arm is warm around my waist. I lean into him as we take the swift, smooth ride upstairs. "Tell me again," I ask, "who's going to be there?"

I'm a little nervous. I mean, it's not every day you meet your boyfriend's family. The fact that they're billionaires? Phew, whatever. I could not care less at this point. But the fact that they're Kade's? Well, I want to make a good impression. I know for sure they've already been talking about me. Colton's confessed. We've only been a couple for a while, but our relationship has been intense.

I mean, you break one guy's leg, and all of a sudden, they're gossiping like a bunch of hens. These guys seem to be very much up in each other's business. Yeah, they work together, but it's so much bigger than that. They have a group text that pings all day long. It's ridiculous, and I desperately want to be added to it.

It's foreign to me, but I love that Kade has it. This big group of unruly men who love him and always have his back. But I know it's because they love him that they're going to be judging me. Looking for flaws. Looking for reasons why I'm not good enough for him.

I wish I could say that I don't care if they like me, but that's not completely true. They sound like a group of cut-throat savages, and I really want in. I want to be in that club. I know I've got Kade, Colton, and Micah on my side, but the others are unknown.

Kade pulls me in closer, pressing his lips to my temple. "Everyone," he says. "You don't need to worry about the guys. They're predisposed to like you because Colton's been raving about you. Ransom though…"

"Right. Ransom thinks I'm going to rob you blind," I say with a smirk.

Kade groans. "He doesn't…well, maybe a little bit. You know my history. He's had to chase off a few women over the years. The ones that really…"

"Dug their claws into you," I finish. I really hate the look on his face right now. Like he's reliving every mistake he's ever made.

I turn into him, wrapping my arms around his waist, pressing my body against his, breast to thigh. I slide my hands down his back until I have nice handfuls of ass. Rising on my tiptoes, I press my mouth against his. "From now on, mine are the only claws that will ever be dug into you," I breathe. "I can promise you that."

He takes my mouth with a grin, his hands tangling in my hair, pulling my head back so he can plunder. I love it when he does that. Makes me want to play pirate and maiden. He can make me play on his plank. He presses me against the wall of the elevator, pushing up, his thigh rising to press against me in just the right…

…And we're falling. Somehow Kade manages to spin us so I land on top of him with an "oomp." My hands immediately go to the back of his head, and I sigh in relief when I don't feel any bumps. Not my best entrance, but again, far from the worst. The Tokyo panties on my head deal was way more embarrassing. Falling out of an elevator while making out with a hot guy? That's kinda awesome. I lean down to take Kade's mouth again, sliding back into my pirate fantasy when the voices penetrate.

"Ohhh, Chad. The Russian athletes are going to lose points for that dismount. It's going to be quite the upset if the Finns take it from behind."

"Taking it from behind is really what it's all about, Bruce. If Dixon is looking for a win here, he'll have to take it hard."

The laughter bursts out of me. Giggling and snorting, I lay my head on Kade's chest, trying to compose myself. But then the third voice joins in.

"Come on, guys. You know Dixon's proven he can take a pounding. He's done it over and over. And he just keeps on coming…and coming."

The fake sports announcer voices, the deadpan delivery have me literally rolling. I tip off Kade, flopping onto my back on the concrete floor, tears streaming down my face.

These idiots.

They're awesome.

Kade's swearing and tugging me to sit up, and I'm absolutely no help, my limbs flopping, unable to do anything but giggle-snort. He finally sighs heavily. I hear him laughing, though, then he scoots behind me, propping me up.

Still laughing, I wipe the tears off my face. When I have myself somewhat under control, I collapse back against his chest, studying the three idiots in front of me.

Colton is there, of course. We've started to spend time together at the Dojo, and I'm happy to report he's just as much of an idiot there. The other two I haven't met yet though I have an inkling that the one wearing the cardigan with his sweats must be Jonas. I mentally slap my own face for imagining him differently. When Kade mentioned he's on the spectrum, I somehow didn't imagine this guy. Someone who would tease his friends. And that's really fucked up. I've got to do better. The other guy, well, I've got no clue, though of course he's hot, even wearing sweats.

"Hey," I say, giving them both a floppy wave. "I'm Becca."

Hot guy smiles. "Nick," he says, then points to the other guy. "That's Jonas." Jonas smiles, briefly meeting my eyes, then turns and walks away.

"Bye Jonas!" I yell. He waves over his shoulder, and I turn my attention to Nick. I swear all these guys came straight out of a fitness magazine. "So which one are you again? What's your superpower?"

He grins, showing off a killer set of dimples. "Ah, beautiful lady…I convince people to give us what we want." His voice is rich, smooth, with a hint of a hispanic accent. I would pay him to read me the naughty parts of my favorite books.

In a heartbeat.

I make a show of fanning myself. "Hey, um…could you say 'her lush thighs pressed against his ears as he lick—'"

"Becca!" Kade yells. "Nick, don't fucking do it." He's glaring at Nick. Nick is laughing, and I still really want him to say it.

The elevator behind us opens suddenly. Micah steps off the elevator, reaching down for a fist bump. "Becca," he says with a smile. Next, another tall guy struggles off the elevator. He's not as tall as Micah and Kade, but I mean, who is? He's wearing a black hoodie and carrying…three giant bags of those colorful kids' ball pit balls.

"Declan," Micah says, winking at me, then pointing to the

guy. Declan finally makes it off the elevator, cursing and swearing, revealing the final two occupants.

It suddenly occurs to me that I should get off the foyer floor and try to act like a grown-up. I stand, smiling, and extend my hand to the next guy off. He looks like he's just come from a GQ shoot. His hair perfectly mussed, his suit still immaculate. His sparkling, dark eyes hinting at his asian ancestry. The resemblance to Jonas is striking—has to be his brother.

"Hi, Zach," I say. "Nice to finally meet you."

His slow smile is killer. His eyes rake me up and down, then he reaches for my hand, bringing it to his mouth, pressing a soft kiss to my palm. He murmurs a hello while I stare at him with wide eyes.

"Woah," I murmur, "I bet you do really well with the ladies. Just line them up like dominoes, don't you?"

He laughs, dropping the playboy act, and shrugs. "I do okay. It's really nice to finally meet you, Becca. Kade's being greedy, keeping you to himself. It's about time you came to family dinner."

"Move it, Romeo," comes a gruff voice.

Zach steps back, and out comes another dark-haired guy in a suit, this one not looking as comfortable in it as Zach. And, of course, he's carrying an armful of skateboards.

Why wouldn't he be?

"Colton!" he yells, looking over my head. "Come and get these fucking things." Then he shifts his eyes down to me, studying me until finally, a small smile crosses his face. "Hi. I'm Maverick." His eyes are kind, but he looks so worn. Is he working too much like Kade was? Or is it something else?

I smile back. "I'm sorry. I know it's lame. I'm sure you've been asked a million times, but—"

He shakes his head, his forehead wrinkling. "Not a nickname. My mom was obsessed with Top Gun."

"Got it. Okay, guy with the coolest name ever, it's really nice to meet you."

We're interrupted by Colton's big body pushing between us. "This is going to be so epic, Mav. You have no idea."

He's hyped up, his words running together. He shoves his ass into my stomach, stepping back, forcing me backward. I grab onto him with my left arm, then snake my right hand under his T-shirt, getting a firm grip on his nipple, twisting till he drops to the floor screaming.

Kade's laughing again, then he steps up behind me. "Looks like you're gonna do just fine, baby. I'll go find you a beer." He presses a quick, hot kiss on my lips, slipping me some tongue before wandering off.

Maverick's staring down at Colt, who's currently cursing me while rolling around, clutching his nipple. His shoulders start to quake. Then the belly laughs roll out of him. He doesn't reach down to help or offer any sympathy. No, he drops the skateboards on top of Colt, steps over him, and wraps a big arm around my shoulders.

"This is gonna be fun," he murmurs.

Maverick steers me out of the foyer the elevator opens to, and my feet stutter-step when I get a look at the penthouse we're in. I swear I've been in smaller stadiums. The whole place has an industrial vibe, with steel and concrete everywhere. The floors are polished concrete. Other than a huge dining room table and a living room setup with three big couches and cozy-looking chairs, there's not much furniture.

It seems so bare, and I don't really get it until Colton rolls past me on a skateboard, the rest of them clutched in his arms. He's not much of a skater, but he manages to stay up, throwing boards at the guys as he goes. Soon Declan, Zach, Kade, and Jonas are skating through the place, spinning and doing other tricks I've seen skaters do.

They shouldn't be that graceful on skateboards, these big

powerful guys. But they are. Though Declan and Nick colliding and crashing to the floor bring some clarity to the vast emptiness of the penthouse. They're a bunch of overgrown kids. Any extra crap in here would end up broken within a day.

Maverick steers me toward the kitchen before excusing himself. I'm pretty sure it's bigger than two garage bays, filled with stainless steel and gleaming countertops. But somehow, the guy standing there makes it look tiny. It's not just his size. He's a big guy for sure, but so are the rest of them. It's his presence. His watchfulness. He's got badass big-brother energy for days.

Honestly, all of them look like they could be related. Dark hair, tall, powerful builds. I wonder if Ransom did it on purpose when he built this family? Like a no blondes allowed type thing?

I lock eyes with him as I circle the island, hopping up to sit on top. He reaches into the fridge, popping the top off a beer and passing it to me with a nod. I take it with a smile, sipping as I look around the spotless space.

"That stove looks brand new," I say, gesturing with my bottle. "Do you not know how to cook either?"

Ransom's eyes don't leave my face. He looks like he's dissecting me, trying to make me squirm. I try to hold it in, but it's just too much.

I snort.

Then I snort some more, and yep, there go the gigglesnorts. Ransom raises an eyebrow, looking at me sternly, which just sets me off again.

"I'm sorry," I say through my giggles. "It's just…you're so cute, all protective and grumpy." I wipe my eyes, sighing, before smiling big at him. Both his eyebrows are raised now, but he doesn't look so carved out of rock anymore. "I get it, dude." I giggle at the way his eyes widen at 'dude.' "You're protective of my guy. I already love you for that. But that shit," I mimic his scowl, "doesn't work on me. If you want to know something, just ask."

He carefully puts his beer down, then leans back against the countertop. The tension in his body is still there, but less.

"Why doesn't it work on you?" he asks.

I shrug. "A combination of things. Having to face down competitors at tournaments, maybe. Possibly facing down a deranged guy with a knife. But more likely?" I pause, sorting carefully through my words. "I've watched someone I love die a slow and painful death. The pain of that…well, someone judging me barely registers."

"Mmm," he hums, looking deep in thought. "Kade is my brother," he rumbles. "I don't want him hurt."

"I get that," I tell him. We stare at each other, the thuds and yells of the guys a racket in the background. It's easy for me to tune out. "Is this where we discuss my intentions?" I ask seriously.

The corner of his mouth twitches. It's brief, but I'll take the win. "Yeah. It's where we discuss what'll happen to you if you fuck him over."

"Fuck him over," I repeat slowly. "What does that mean exactly?"

"I mean," he says deliberately, "that if you hurt him. If you steal from him. If you lie to him. You. Deal. With. Me."

I flex my toes, thinking about his threat. "Sounds fair," I say with a wide smile.

He drops his arms and straightens. "Just like that?" he asks suspiciously.

"Yep," I say, giving him a shit-eating grin. "I have no plans to do anything like that. It's not who I am, and eventually, you'll see that. I don't cheat. I don't lie. I don't steal—except once. But that bitch deserved it." That dog is way better off now too. Eating homemade stew for supper and sleeping in his own twin bed.

"What's your angle then?"

"My angle…" I trail off, more than a little confused.

His mouth firms. "Everyone wants something, Becca. What do you want?"

"Oh," I say quietly.

"Why do you look so sad?" he asks, brows arrowed down.

"I guess you're right, everyone does have an angle, but I would never have put it that way. The fact that you do makes me…hurt for you a bit."

"Hurt for me?" He raises his eyebrows. "You, the girl with no home, living in her car, hurts for me? Have you looked around you?"

My laugh makes his eyebrows dance. "That won't work on me either. I'm not ashamed of my situation when I met Kade. I'm not ashamed of it now." I let my smile fall away. "You look at people, and you see them playing an angle. I don't pretend to really understand everything you guys went through growing up, but I guess that perspective worked for you. Maybe because it was more about survival. But I don't see people that way."

"But you want something," he says flatly.

"Of course I do! If you think about it, about where I come from, it's not that hard to figure out."

I see his gears spinning, then the slow, dawning realization. He looks past me, watching his brothers. "You want this," he says, still studying them.

I turn to watch them, too, giggling when Jonas and Declan collide and land on top of each other.

"Yeah," I say when his eyes shift to me. "I grew up with the best dad in the world. I know what it's like to have someone in my life that I can depend on. And I thought that I had built a community—but it wasn't strong enough. When things got tough…they were gone. I got to a place where no one in this world loved me. I had acquaintances. People who liked me. But no one who truly loved me and wanted to be there for me."

"So yeah, I want all of this. I want to have roots. Connections. I want to be loved. I want to be part of a family again." I smile at him. "I love Kade. I won't trade him for anything. But I would really, really, like some big brothers too." The ice in Ransom's eyes is starting to thaw. "I don't expect it to happen overnight. I know I have to earn that place. But I'm really fucking persistent. And super loveable. Before you know it, you'll think of me as an annoying little sister."

"You're not going anywhere, are you?" he says finally, the hint of a grin peeking through.

"Nope," I say, beaming.

"We'll see." Hiding his smile, he pulls out his phone. "I've got my eye on you." Then he nods and walks toward the elevator.

He's going to be the best big brother. I just know it.

Kade comes in, pushing between my legs until he's got me wrapped around him. "You okay?" he asks, his mouth brushing my neck.

"Yeah," I say, tipping my head to give him better access. "I love your brother." I feel his smile against my skin.

"Did he give you the 'I'm watching you' speech?"

"Yep," I say with a laugh. "He was super intimidating and growly."

"Yeah, you seem totally fucking intimidated," he says, laughing.

"We understand each other. He'll come around in time."

"Good," he murmurs.

"Food's here!" Ransom yells from the elevator. The guys dive off their skateboards and rush to grab bags of food. Kade grabs my ass, pulling me off the island into his arms as the bags and the men descend on us.

The meal is organized chaos. Everyone yelling and shoving. Complaining. But there's also a ton of teasing and laughing. Even Maverick, with the tired eyes, looks energized by it.

It's toward the end of the meal that I finally ask the question I can't believe no one else has asked.

"Declan," I say, watching him scoop up the last of his noodles, "what are you going to do with all those balls?"

He freezes, fork halfway to his mouth. His smile is evil, and it sends a thrill down my spine. Colton is already giggling at the other end of the table. He knows what's up. This is going to be good. "Hungry Hippos," he says casually, shoving the rest of his food in his mouth.

My eyes widen, excitement flooding my body as I scan the room. Of course! The skateboards, the laundry basket, but… "Where are the other baskets?" I ask with a frown.

Declan freezes. He glances around wildly before slumping in his chair. "We fucking forgot them," he says, covering his face.

"No," I moan, dropping my head into my hands. "Wait!" I yell, jumping up from my chair.

While the rest of the guys watch, confused, I grab Declan by the hoodie and yank him out of his chair. I drag him over to the large shelving unit in the living room, slapping the back of Colton's head as we pass and head straight to the decorative baskets.

"They could work, right?" I ask, grabbing one and looking inside. It's filled with candy.

Declan grabs it, dumping the candy on the couch, his excitement rising again. "You're a genius! Yes, they'll work." We grab baskets, madly dumping the contents onto the couch. More candy, some car parts, about twenty random socks, and a bunch of paper airplanes later, we've got a giant pile of expensive baskets.

"Alright!" Declan screams, his arms raised in victory. He dashes back to the table. "Five teams of two. Go!" Then he runs back to me. "Becca's my partner!" he hollers over his shoulder.

I grab the hair tie off my wrist, pulling my hair up into a

tight bun. "Let's kick some ass," I mutter, slapping him on the ass as I walk toward the skateboards.

"What the fuck is hungry hippos, and why the fuck do you get to play with my girl?" Kade's grumpy voice makes me smile.

Declan replies, "It's a game of champions, man. And because I called dibs." He dodges out of reach when Kade swipes at him, cackling as he runs to the other side of the room and up the metal staircase. He stops when he's a few steps up. "Listen up, dipshits. This is how this is gonna go. Becca, grab the gear." I grab a skateboard and basket, then run to join him with a whoop.

I might be a little excited.

"The goal is to get as many balls as you can into your big basket," he says, gesturing to the bigger of the baskets we just emptied, "by using your little basket."

All the guys, except Colt, who looks manic, seem bored until I lay on the skateboard on my stomach, a smaller basket extended in front of me. Then I raise my legs so Declan can get a good grip. "Now picture a giant pile of balls in the center of a circle, with five people on skateboards. Then we just…"

He proceeds to shove me forward and back frantically as I capture imaginary balls. I look up to see dawning smiles and gleeful faces. Even Ransom is smiling. I have a feeling big, serious Ransom is going to have a blast.

It's a shit show but in the best possible way. We're all vicious, none of the guys seem to care that I'm a girl, pushing and shoving me just as much as each other. I love it. I hand out a few pinches and barely avoid a concussion.

It's awesome.

Declan is singing the team song we made up before we started. "Declan and Becca, kicking your ass. K-I-C-K-I-N-G.

First comes victory, then comes nurples. Then comes Becca with a lady boner."

We wrote it in two minutes. Don't judge.

And I was right. Ransom is laughing, pushing a screaming Nick on the skateboard. And in the end, of course, Declan and I win. There really was no doubt in my mind. We were clearly the most exceptional team. And if there's one thing I know how to do, it's win.

We end up lying on the polished concrete floors, laughing and drinking. The guys are still shit-talking and telling stories. I lay there, smiling, as I listen to this family, this family that I'm going to make my own, so fucking grateful that my shitty car broke down all those months ago.

****

Thank you so much for reading Kade. Micah and Holly's story continues in *Micah: A Brash Brothers Billionaire Romance*

Want a little more Kade & Becca? Grab a bonus scene from my website authorjennamyles.com

ABOUT THE AUTHOR

So apparently, not everyone has entire worlds and a whole cast of made up characters living in their head. I bought my first book on how to write romance fifteen years ago.

And did absolutely nothing with it.

Until one day, tired of all my wishing and doubting, I sat down and started writing. The plan was to prove to myself that I sucked. Turns out, not only do I not suck, I tell really great stories.

And those people who live in my head? They've been desperate to get out. In my other life I'm a single mother by choice, through adoption and as a foster parent. As a result, neurodivergent kids and kids from hard places have a special spot in my heart

Jenna

facebook.com/authorjennamyles
instagram.com/authorjennamyles
tiktok.com/jennalovesromance

23451422R00137